Centurionman
A Collection of Short Stories

Andrew Campbell-Kearsey

Spinetinglers
PUBLISHING

Centurionman – A Collection of Short Stories
By Andrew Campbell-Kearsey

ISBN - 978-1-906657-15-4

Spinetinglers Elite Publishing
22 Vestry Road
Co. Down
BT23 6HJ
UK
www.spinetinglerspublishing.com

Cover designed by Michael Halliday

Andrew is a former headteacher from London. He now lives and writes in Brighton. The first time he ever felt like a writer was in 2009. He won the Ilkley Literary Festival Short Story Competition and had the opportunity to read out his winning story to a theatre full of people. When the audience listened attentively and laughed at the right bits, Andrew thought he might be on to something. He has written over two hundred short stories. Thorny Devil Productions have selected three as the basis for a series of short films. The first, 'Shrinking Violet', premiered in August 2013 at the HollyShorts Film Festival in Hollywood, Los Angeles.

He has learned the only way to get a reaction to a story is to get it out there. His long-suffering partner is in an impossible situation. If he says he likes the story, it could be out of politeness. If he dares criticise, then Andrew is known to go several times around the block on his huffy bike. Andrew is currently putting the finishing touches to the umpteenth edit of his second novel, before sending it off to agents and publishers.

Writing under the penname Centurionman, Andrew has been crowned the winner of the monthly Spinetinglers.co.uk Short Story Competition on several occasions, and is a regular in the top 5. His success on the site lead to a publishing offer, and the aptly entitled Centurionman - A Collection of Short Stories was born.

To Steve

Table of Contents

Foreword

I have been writing for several years. In a former life I used to be a primary head teacher. I have exchanged inspections, targets and budgets for what I enjoy; I make things up.

I love the format of a short story and I'm delighted that Spinetinglers are publishing this ebook. I'm particularly interested in writing from the viewpoint of the unreliable narrator.

A couple of my stories have been made into films by Thorny Devil Productions. It's a strange experience to watch the characters I've created talking on a screen. An adaptation of 'Dangerous Precedent', called *A Quiet Courage*, was shown at the Cannes Film Festival. 'Shrinking Violet' premiered at the Hollywood Shorts film festival in August 2013.

Thanks for buying this. I hope there will be many more to follow.

Centurionman/Andrew C-K
July 2013

Celebrity Status

A face transplant seems like an attractive option. I'm sure that the surgeons wouldn't perform the operation on a whim. I would have to become horribly disfigured; maybe an accident with matches or acid. I could read up on dog psychology and turn next door's Alsatian into a mauling monster. Here's my stop.

It's not that far to my front door but it's touch and go whether I'll get back by the time the Heavens open. My headscarf won't offer much protection. The plastic carrier bag handles are cutting into my fingers but at five pence each I made do with only four. The door keys are in the last of the pockets I check, which means the rain won this round. If only the council would come and repair this porch. Apparently, arson damage is no longer a priority for them. I feel another letter coming on. But what's the point? They never bother to answer them.

Coming home to an empty home has its advantages. I can eat a ready meal straight from the container, watching my favourite programmes. I can't believe the way they carry on, swearing at members of their own family. The things people will do to get on television. Some people just have no shame. I've tried the marriage thing. Ditched the name but kept the photographs. They're in the drawer over there. I don't have them up. Reminds me of how much weight I've put on. Don't even know where he lives now. I never had to nag him, like I hear some of them on this estate doing. I'm past blushing at the language they come out with around here. It's a rough old neighbourhood but beggars can't be choosers.

The answering machine is flashing. Only one message. It wasn't too long ago when it would always be full. So many ignorant people out there; I don't know how they got my number. The journalists were worse, pretending they were my friends. I changed my number when I moved.

I press *play* with some trepidation; old habits die hard. That's a relief; the message is from Janine. I quite like her. She was kind when I met her last week. I got the impression she felt sorry for me. It makes a change to have another person on my side. She wants to know if I can confirm my appointment with her tomorrow morning. That's sweet of her. I suppose she doesn't realise I hardly have a list of pressing engagements. I'll give her a quick ring now before *Countdown*.

The GP has been reluctant to prescribe me with any sleeping tablets. I turn off the bedside lamp and my brain starts working overtime. If I tune in to some phone-in show on the radio I'll be up all night listening to those ranting nutters. They make me laugh; getting all uptight about the most trivial things. I used to get mentioned sometimes. They'd talk as if they knew me.

I hear the letterbox rattle. There's a storm but I can't take chances. I've had smoke detectors fitted but it could be too late by the time the fire has spread to my bedroom. My feet stick to the lino in parts as I pad along the hall to the front door. It was just the wind this time.

Celebrity Status

*****

I'm sitting at my kitchen table at half past seven. I used to cook my husband a proper fry-up breakfast every morning. I expect his arteries are grateful we're not together anymore. Only three and a half hours until my appointment. The bus into town should take about twenty minutes so I have plenty of time to kill. I should take up a hobby. Janine suggested an evening class. But it's too soon. She's got no idea what it's like to be me. Although it's begun to die down, it's never going to go away completely. I'd take up knitting, but the wool's so dear these days. I don't think there'll be too many takers for children's clothes made by me.

I reckon I could do more to make this place look smarter. The council said it was temporary but I figure I'll be here for a while. I was in a bed and breakfast for the first few months. I kept getting moved on. I don't think I'll bother decorating. It's only me here and I don't get any visitors nowadays.

It's almost time to go. I feel anxious about leaving my home every morning. I close my eyes momentarily as I open the door then step outside. I turn to lock it. There's no graffiti today. I just ignore it now when somebody points me out to their friend. It's happening less and less.

I arrive characteristically early. I sit in the waiting room. The magazines are not new but recent enough to have nothing on their covers about me. I can't imagine why any celebrity would court publicity. I'm not sure but the receptionist seems to be staring at me.

My father would have been amazed that his daughter had become a woman who turned heads. He never thought I would amount to much. I went through a phase of changing my appearance. I bought a range of headscarves from local charity shops. I'd never set foot in one before, but needs must. I didn't think I was the type for hats but I have quite a collection now. I don't bother with disguises any more. Nobody has spat at me for a couple of weeks.

I look at the woman behind the desk, concentrating on her computer screen. That could have been me. She might be five years younger than me but if things had been different I might have fathomed how to use one of those and I would have had lots of opportunities. I could have been the secretary to some high flying executive. I could have travelled and sent people postcards from all over, just to make them jealous. Then they would see that I had made something of my life.

Janine pops her head out of her office, sees me, smiles and beckons me to come in.

"Good morning, Sarah. Is it alright for me to call you by your first name?"

"Yes." I like the fact that she asked.

"How was your journey here?"

I see this for the small talk it is and give her a few details about my uneventful bus trip. I could have added a few fictional characters and incidents to liven things up, but I'd better stick to the truth.

"So, tell me Sarah, in your own words, how you are feeling."

I pause. "Things are calming down. The craziness of last year has passed."

Janine says nothing; just nods. I am meant to continue. She feels the need to prompt. "So, what are your plans?"

"I'm thinking of looking for a job. That's if anyone would want me."

I expect Janine to say something reassuring to me but she keeps it factual.

"What experience do you have?"

"Mostly shop work. Don't think I'd be a good advertisement at the moment, though. Some customers are bound to recognise me."

"How about training, starting a course?"

"No. I'm done with all that. Didn't have a great time at school. Besides, I need to earn some money. I'm not used to living off benefits."

Another pause.

"I'm sure you want to know why I did it."

"If that's what you want to talk about."

"The truth is. I'm not sure. It just got out of hand. After I made the first call to the police, I lost control and there was no stopping it."

"Did you like the attention?"

"At first. The policewoman they sent was very nice. I was impressed. She was sitting down in my living room, drinking tea, twenty minutes after the call. She asked me so many questions. I almost didn't recognise the words that came out of my own mouth. It was like I had rehearsed it. She explained to me that two of her colleagues would carry out a thorough search of the house for any evidence that might help them. I knew what she really meant. I was obviously their number one suspect. They just found what I wanted them to find."

Janine is scribbling furiously, yet still looking intently at me. I don't know how she manages to keep her writing on the lines of her pad.

"It must have taken a lot of planning."

"Not really. All I had to do was have a convincing photograph, buy a few toys and have a suitcase of girl's clothes."

"Where did you get the idea from?"

"It just came to me. The librarian showed me how to look for photographs on the computer. I made her write down the buttons I should press. I picked one that looked a bit like me, not too pretty. I knew I couldn't pass her off as my own. That's where I had the idea of saying I was looking after my niece while her parents had a second honeymoon."

"You must have known that people would find out."

"Yes, but I swept that under the carpet. It all went my way to start with. After I said that she'd been missing for a few hours they didn't waste any time. They took my word for everything. I named my niece after my first doll."

"Imaginary niece, Sarah, she wasn't real. You made her up."

"Yes, I know that. The story got on to the news that evening. Neighbours I'd hardly spoken to knocked at the door, offering to help. There was a search party of over fifty people that night, poring over the park where I'd said she'd last been seen. I was worried the librarian would remember the picture of the girl's face I'd printed off. But she didn't. The press conference was like a dream. I didn't plan to break down in front of the cameras. That just happened. The policewoman had to take over from me. I should have taken some of the money journalists were offering me. I even had agents calling me, wanting to represent me. A local businessman put up the money for a reward. It was more than my house was worth. After thirty-six hours, my mother came forward to let them know that I was an only child. It all began to unravel. I couldn't give the police the name of the hotel where my sister was staying. There were no witnesses who had seen me with an eight year old girl, or any child. I confessed to the same policewoman. She wasn't so kind this time. I was arrested for wasting police time. The tone of the headlines in the tabloids changed overnight. I was labelled the most hated woman in Britain. Total strangers were on television, giving their opinions of why I had done it. Everyone had a theory: it was because I hadn't achieved much at school, my husband had left me or I had always wanted a child. Take your pick."

"How was the trial?"

"All a blur, even though it's less than a year ago. I was driven to court in one of those police vans with the blacked out windows. The scariest thing was people banging on the side of the van. The noise was terrible, the shouting...I thought they would get in. After that, the trial was nothing. I pleaded guilty and said sorry at every opportunity. That's why my barrister said I got off so lightly. I ended up with community service. Didn't mind the work, just that nobody talked to me. Plus I have to come and speak with people like you."

"Are you sorry for what happened now?"

"Of course I am. I wish I'd never been caught."

That stops her scribbling.

Aspirational Fruit

Julia checked her appointments. They were stacking up. She had a ten thirty, an eleven o'clock and a twelve fifteen. Parking was always a nightmare on a Saturday. It was just as well she'd found that blue disability parking permit. She didn't know how other people managed.

She could still recall the look that traffic warden had given her a few weeks ago. She'd managed to squeeze her two-seater into a disabled parking bay near the town hall. She was running late for a viewing and hated to keep other people waiting. It looked bad. As she emerged from her car, the warden was standing at the other side of the road watching her. He was clearly wondering why an apparently able bodied woman in her mid-thirties with an extremely expensive sports car was entitled to this prime parking spot. Fortunately Julia had seen *The Usual Suspects* recently and mimicked Kevin Spacey's limp admirably.

Once she'd turned the corner, she sprinted to the second floor loft conversion that promised 'sea views and a 21st century living experience'. It was a poky, little studio flat that required plenty of neck-craning to spy the microscopic sliver of sea that was sandwiched between the two imposing houses opposite. But the visit hadn't been entirely wasted.

Julia was checking her appearance in the hallway mirror when a text came through from the office. There was now a fourth appointment booked in for one thirty. She was certainly going to have a busy Saturday.

*****

The first appointment was a complete waste of time. She hated it when the owners were present. They always said the wrong thing and were somewhere on the needy to smarmy continuum. This couple were the worst. They were clearly so desperate to flog their home that they were making so many preposterous claims about the place; about is energy efficiency, its proximity to all amenities and how fantastic the neighbours were. Why did they want to move then?

The second was a flat that had a funny smell that seemed to relocate to whichever room Julia was in. *It would be a struggle to sell this to anybody at all*, Julia thought.

As she walked around the fourth home of the day she somehow managed to suppress a groan when she entered the dining room. There on the table was a glass bowl. On its own, it would not have been offensive. It had a pleasing enough pattern. But it was filled to the brim with one of Julia's pet hates. The owners had evidently been shopping that very morning and ensured that they had cornered the market in 'aspirational fruit'.

Julia wished on this occasion that the owners were present. She would take them to one side and explain the principle of 'Less Is More'. Kumquats nestling amongst Sharon fruits, *I ask you*, she thought. Nestling in among the orange hues she spotted the green skinned quinces. To the more casual observer these may have been mistaken for common or garden pears; but not Julia. She was well trained in spotting the exotic creatures of the fruit world.

When she arrived home, she emptied her coat pockets. It wasn't a great haul. The spoon she simply would add to her growing cutlery collection. The ceramic cupcake from the second home was a little risky. There were over twenty on display on the kitchen window-ledge, and there was a danger that collectors always knew exactly how many they owned. Julia couldn't help but think that was such a petty trait. The door stop would come in handy however. Julia needed one of those and she never knew what type of shop would stock them. Besides, her job kept her busy and the weekends were so often taken up with property viewings.

The only item of value she had stolen had been from the aspirational fruit buyers. They deserved it. It was quite reckless, Julia supposed. The brooch had been on the dressing table. But their stupidity needed to be punished.

*****

The following weekend she had another set of viewings in a neighbouring town. Julia kept fastidious notes on which estate agency businesses she had used in the past. Repetition might lead to slip-ups. Julia was professional in her approach.

She had three visits planned with three different agents. She could have worn the same outfit as the previous week as she would be meeting new people. However, she would know, so she wore her favourite charcoal grey business suit. Despite the fact that it was the middle of winter, she donned a pair of designer sunglasses. It was just a couple of weeks until Christmas but the sun was making an unseasonally strong appearance. When she'd made the appointments over the phone during the week, the agents had failed to hide the fact their excitement. Mid-December was a slack time for property sales, and this year particularly so in this time of global meltdown. Julia seemed such an attractive client. She had her story well rehearsed. She was a cash buyer with absolutely nothing to sell. She had recently returned from a lucrative contract abroad and was looking for properties up to six hundred thousand. Last year she used to tell people her limit was four hundred thousand but she liked the way that the staff treated her when she increased her potential buying power. They became especially attentive.

She drove for twenty minutes along the coast road to the neighbouring seaside town. There was precious little traffic on the road. As usual, she would meet the estate agent at the property. They often employed Saturday staff for the weekend viewings at peak times of the year. They were the careless ones. She was always free to roam around unsupervised. This made her borrowing ever so easy. That's what she called it. She'd never decided upon a time when she would return the objects that she borrowed from the homes she viewed.

The short drive for Julia made all the difference in property terms. Her notional money would go a lot further here. She slowed down to view the house and then parked a little way down the road from the house. She had a full ten minutes to spare. She re-read the particulars. Whoever wrote these ones must have had a degree in English literature.

She could observe the owners of the property pulling out of the drive with their two children in their people carrier. Julia did so hate gas-guzzling cars. This wasn't a great start for the hopeful house-sellers. The value of the object that Julia intended to borrow went up in price. Julia thought she'd make the man pay this time. He'd obviously chosen the offending car. With luck, there would be some cufflinks on display.

She could see from her car's mirror the back of the estate agent as he wrestled with the double lock. Julia would allow him a few minutes to prepare the house for her viewing. Julia pictured him plumping cushions and deciding which lights to leave on. She could afford to take her time over this one as the next viewing was in an hour and a quarter and only five minutes away.

Julia walked up the garden path and rang on the doorbell. Her broad smile evaporated as soon as the door was opened.

"Good morning, Ms Jones."

Julia attempted to sound cheerful but she could tell from the look on his face that he was puzzled. She shook his hand and announced, "I'm in a little bit of a hurry so could we make this quick please."

Julia made the calculation that he may not remember her. Her eidetic memory meant that she could recall the date and time that he had last shown her around a property. He had shown countless people around a variety of homes in between. Maybe she would be lucky and he would not recognise her.

They were in the kitchen when he turned to her,

"Excuse me for saying this, but you seem terribly familiar."

"I can't imagine why." She instantly regretted responding so tersely. It didn't seem to bother him and he continued.

"I've just transferred from the main office in Brighton. I could have sworn I showed you around a penthouse apartment overlooking the Marina."

"I can assure you, young man, that we have never met before as it is patently clear that I am looking for a large family home, hence my presence here. I can't imagine why you think you have shown me a flat before. It certainly does not meet my family's requirements. My time is limited and valuable and precious. I am fairly secure in the knowledge that our paths have never previously crossed."

The remainder of the viewing was conducted monosyllabically. Julia was in such a hurry to leave that she almost forgot to borrow the cufflinks that were in a small dish at the bedside table.

She could hardly remember the drive home. She'd cancelled the two other viewings. Back at home she found a brown paper bag and took deep breaths. After a few minutes, she was able to breathe normally and her heart stopped racing. She added the newly acquired cufflinks to her growing collection.

A glass of wine and the classical strains of Radio Three further helped to calm her nerves.

An hour later Julia decided to enter the day's events into her online blog. She took great delight in describing the interior design faults of each homeowner. Her followers would no doubt be disappointed that she only reported the one viewing for that day. She would have to ensure that the comments were especially vitriolic. No half measures today. There was a knock at the door. She wasn't expecting anybody, but carol-singers could be so persistent.

"Good afternoon Madam. May we come in?"

After Julia had been shown their ID cards, she allowed them in. The two police officers followed her through to her conservatory.

"How can I help you officers?"

The older of the two produced a notebook and read from it.

"We received a call from a young man a few hours ago who recognised you as a former client. He showed you around a flat last year and afterwards the owners reported a lost necklace, presumed stolen. You gave a different address so the investigating officer was unable to follow up in his inquiries. You gave a false address today but fortunately the young man committed your number plate to memory and we traced you. The owners of the house you viewed today have informed us that a pair of antique cufflinks is missing. Do you happen to know their whereabouts?"

Julia blushed and tried to cover her reaction with a voice of great indignation.

"I live alone officers and I can assure you that I have no need for cufflinks. I believe that all of our time is being wasted."

"You won't mind us having a look around then, Ms Goddard?"

They didn't wait for an answer. Within five minutes they had located the cufflinks, the necklace and many other incongruous items. She'd left her laptop open and they were fascinated by that day's entry.

"I can explain, officers."

"I'm sure you can Ms Goddard. Perhaps it will be a little easier down at the station."

"Please don't bother to read me my rights."

She gestured to a framed certificate on the wall. They both moved nearer to inspect Julia's law degree and the photograph next to it of her in her judge's robes. The newspaper clipping read *Britain's Youngest Ever High Court Judge*.

Only Scribbling

His hands were sticky. The vanilla ice cream had leaked through the soggy cornet. He licked his fingers and then rubbed his palms on his shorts. His mother always had an endless supply of handkerchiefs in her handbag. But he knew better than to interrupt her when she was on the telephone. He could see her through the red lattice-work door of the telephone box. She's been in there for ages, talking to Uncle Charlie.

Johnny sat on the wall at the edge of the beach. He swung his feet. They didn't quite touch the ground. There was a small pebble in his left sandal. It must have worked its way in through the cut-out pattern of the leather. He tried to ease it out with his finger but the fabric of his sock made it difficult. He couldn't take it off as he hadn't mastered the buckle yet. His mother would have to sort it out for him.

He sat patiently, every so often turning to witness his mother still talking on the phone. He was not close enough to hear actual words. But he could tell she was raising her voice.

There was a patch of pinkish-red sand further along the promenade. Johnny had seen people play a game with silver balls there before. Today there was just one person there: an elderly man, dressed in layers of seemingly heavy and baggy clothes and wearing a hand-knitted woolly hat. The man held a rake in his hands and was making patterns in the reddish sand. He was concentrating very hard and his actions were slow. Johnny wanted to see what the man was drawing in the sand. He climbed down from the wall and walked the fifty yards to the edge of the sandy area. The young boy tried to make sense of the series of swirls and circles. The man put down his rake and pulled out a brush from one of his carrier bags. He knelt down and repaired his picture, erasing the footprints a leadless dog had just made. Johnny tilted his head to get a better understanding of what he was witnessing. His teacher would have called this only scribbling. She never liked it when Johnny painted patterns. She always asked, 'What's it supposed to be?' The man had added some shells and pebbles to where the circles intersected, but he didn't have enough. Fortunately Johnny had his bucket with him. He walked over to the man and offered him the now full bucket. The man wordlessly accepted and placed it on the ground. He knelt down, inspected the contents, then selected a smooth round stone from the top. He stood up and gazed at the pattern in the sand for some moments. Then he carefully placed the stone firmly in the sand. He returned to the bucket to consider his next choice. Johnny suddenly heard his mother's voice.

"I've read about men like you! What are you doing with my son's bucket? I should report you to the police."

She grabbed Johnny's hand and ignored his pleas to retrieve the bucket. She pulled him in the direction of where their car was parked on the seafront. Johnny turned and saw the man standing expressionless, clutching the bucket.

"What have I told you about talking to strangers? You should never have wandered off like that. I've been looking for you everywhere. I didn't know what to think."

Johnny knew the best thing was to hang his head down and not answer back. He didn't mention his sandal, even though his foot was beginning to hurt.

"You've completely ruined today. I bought you that new bucket and spade. What on earth were you doing talking to that strange little man? Dressed up like that on a day like today. Simply boiling. I'm taking you straight home now. I can't imagine when he last had a bath."

"But I thought we were having lunch with Uncle Charlie? He was going to show me his new cigarette cards."

"Stop whining, will you. You know how I hate it. We're going home and that's it. Besides, your Uncle Charlie's busy today. Just wait until I tell your father how you nearly gave me a heart attack today by running off."

Johnny looked up as his mother and saw smudged black lines around her eyes.

*****

Nothing was said about the trip to the seaside at the dinner table that evening. His mother seemed to have forgotten about the whole episode. She listened attentively as her husband recounted his day at the office. She even laughed when Johnny's father did his impression of his boss again. Johnny loved to see his mother happy.

*****

A few weeks later, tucked up in bed, Johnny eavesdropped on his parents.

"I'll take the boy down to the coast tomorrow. The sea air will do him the world of good."

His father hadn't even replied, but had just grunted from behind his newspaper.

Johnny found it difficult to sleep. A whole day out with his mother. Alone together. He would make sure he behaved himself this time.

*****

Bumper to bumper in traffic, Johnny was impatient to get to the beach. She'd bought him a new bucket and spade. No mention of the previous ones. She sat in a deckchair while he played in the sand. Her headscarf and fancy sunglasses made her look rather glamorous in Johnny's eyes. There were several other children playing nearby, but Johnny preferred to work on his own. He was industriously digging out a moat when his mother walked over to him, knelt down and whispered, "I'm just going to call Uncle Charlie. See if he can meet us for lunch. Don't go wandering off. Be a good boy."

Johnny was engrossed in his castle construction. His mother returned a few minutes later with an enormous smile. "He's meeting us at the end of the pier. He's treating us to fish and chips." She didn't wait for Johnny to complete his task. She made him stand up and dabbed at his hands with her handkerchief to remove most of the sand. "You'll do," she said taking his hand. As they walked briskly along the promenade Johnny noticed the familiar stretch of red sand. The same man was there. His patterns were even more intricate. Johnny tried to stop and work out what he was working on but his mother's pace did not falter. He had to run to catch up with her.

*****

Uncle Charlie always put his mother in a good mood. She laughed most with him. She didn't mind when Johnny asked for a second glass of Coke.

"Let the boy have a third and a fourth," his Uncle Charlie said. "I tell you what Johnny, I have the most amazing set of cigarette cards to show you at home. That's if your mother can be persuaded."

Johnny did not have to try terribly hard. The three of them walked back to his house. It was just off the seafront. Johnny knew it well from previous visits.

After Johnny had studied the set of cigarette cards, Uncle Charlie offered him a glass of lemonade. "Go and play out in the garden and I'll bring it out to you."

Johnny loved this garden. It was smaller than his at home, but it had tall pampas grass at the back that made him feel like he was in the jungle and a sundial his Uncle had told him belonged once to King Arthur.

Uncle Charlie stepped into the garden. "Your mother's got one of her headaches. You know what women can be like.' Uncle Charlie laughed at this and carried on. 'Be a good sport and play out here for a while. Your mother's going to be upstairs resting." He handed Johnny some coins. "A little something for the piggy-bank." He went back inside the house, leaving Johnny alone.

When his mother came out into the garden later she seemed to have lost her headache. "Come along Johnny, time to go. We don't want to overstay our welcome, do we?"

Uncle Charlie made a big show of shaking Johnny's hand and kissing his mother on each cheek. "Until next time," he called after them as they walked away. Suddenly Johnny's mother looked unhappy. He was surprised to see her looking so sad and worried what he might have done to upset her. She said nothing as they walked towards the car. In the back seat Johnny noticed that his mother had lost something.

"Mummy, one of your earrings is missing. Shall we go back and look for it?"

There was a pause. His mother sniffed and he could see in the mirror that she was crying. He wanted to try and cheer her up.

"Daddy will be pleased to see us."

This didn't seem to make her any happier. After a couple of minutes she reapplied her eye make-up in the mirror and announced that they were heading home. Johnny needed no encouragement to read and he knew better than to distract his mother while she was driving.

He wasn't looking up when the crash happened. Therapists would later tell him that blacking out had been his body's young way of dealing with the horror.

*****

Johnny died that day and I was born. My dad couldn't cope with me. He would come into my bedroom and not know what to say. Apparently I reminded him of her. I kept asking about my mother and when she was coming home. Eventually I was sent off to stay with my grandparents. They were ready for any outbursts, but I was the model of politeness and good manners.

It wasn't until I was studying for my A-levels that things fell apart. I stopped communicating totally and changed from studious adolescent to lifeless young man. Of course they brought the specialists in and my grandparents decided I would benefit from a residential placement.

I remember my granddad driving me to the large converted house that would become my home. My grandmother decided at the last minute that she couldn't face it. I don't know whether she couldn't face 'it' or me. Once the man on duty had seen the letter and made sure we were who we were supposed to be he made a telephone call and raised the barrier to the entrance gate.

We were met by a man from the big house, who smiled broadly and said, "Welcome. I'm sure that your stay here will be most beneficial."

He went to shake my hand but I refused to recognise or respond to him. The man turned to my grandfather who was struggling with the cases. "Let me help you with those."

The older man declined, as there were only two bags.

"Travelling light, I see." An awkward silence followed.

Up in my room, I sat at the desk in front of the window. My grandfather had made his excuses and left. He never liked to leave his wife alone for long. The man who had welcomed us on the steps knocked on the door shortly afterwards.

"Settling in alright? That's the spirit. I want you to think of this place as your home now. At least for a few months. It might say *hospital* on the sign outside but I prefer to view this place as a home. Your home." He went on to explain how the tight security was for my benefit and how I would only get out from the experience what I was willing to put in. He also mentioned meal times and laundry arrangements.

So my life was to be compartmentalised into stuff that was good for me and the routine of a prison cell. I heard him speaking, but took no notice. Instead I took out my favourite crayons and a large pad of white paper and began to draw. Twenty-two of the colours remained unused and full-length. I only used the pink and red ones, holding them together to form circular patterns on the paper. They had been worn down to become little more than stubs. I'd tried to communicate with my grandparents when I'd finished with these two colours, by silently returning the rest of the box of crayons. They quickly learned that the only way to satisfy me was to provide me with a new set. But I only ever used two colours.

The man was speaking again. "I'll leave you to your artwork Johnny. Lunch is at a quarter to one."

I like to think that he returned to his office and tried to find some significance in my pink and red circles. He'll never know that those circles represented happiness and my past. How could he? I was only scribbling.

Dying to Speak

They think I can't hear them. There are two of them in the other room. I don't know their names. They come and go whenever they please. Probably going through my things right now. Even with the television blaring out, using my precious electricity, I can pick out their words. 'Not long to go' and 'a few days at the most'. One of them is coming. I'd better play the patient.

The lumpen creature comes into my bedroom with a small plastic container and a glass of water. At least I won't have to use the stuff that's stagnating in the jug by my bed. It's been there since yesterday lunchtime. I may get to taste fresh water for a change. I bet she didn't run the tap though.

I've closed my eyes. I'm desperate to sit upright in the bed and scream 'Boo!' - but my body won't let me. I pretend to come to. In my head, I say thank you to her as she hands me the pills. But the garbled sounds that come from my throat are straight out of a David Attenborough special.

This one's not so bad. She plumps up my pillows. Perhaps I should begin to stockpile my medication. I could always feign taking them and let them think I'm following doctor's orders. Then one morning, one of them would come in and find my cold body hideously contorted. I saw a documentary once on what an overdose can do. It's not pretty.

I can't move my legs or right arm, but I don't feel I'm on the way out. I may have totally lost the power of speech and only see out of one eye. The visual effect is quite kaleidoscopic. I misjudge distances. My former mother-in-law used to reel out trite expressions such as 'Many a slip twixt cup and lip'. I'll have to concede this to the old witch; it's rooted in fact. My pyjama jacket is the sodden evidence. But I don't feel as if I'm at death's door. Is this what it feels like to be dying? I thought I'd feel more at peace. Instead little things have taken on gigantic proportions. I can't tell you how irksome I find the sight of my dressing gown hanging limply from the back of my bedroom door. Don't they know the purpose of hangers? Maybe they haven't been on that particular training course yet.

There's the doorbell. The first thing to happen is the television goes off. It must be somebody further up the pecking order. I'm right. It's the doctor. The two laughingly, misnamed care assistants are transformed into 21st century Florence Nightingales. He appears at my bedside, godlike, flanked by his angels of mercy. He asks me questions but doesn't expect me to answer. He must see the confusion in my eyes. His sidekicks tell of my distress and outbursts. What liars they are! No wonder they can't look me in the face. He announces that he'll give me something to make me feel more comfortable. I don't expect his slim briefcase will be holding a pair of size eleven fluffy slippers for me. Instead he produces a syringe. I wish he'd chosen the dead arm to inject. I can't even form the sound 'ow' properly.

*****

I have no idea what the time is. The curtains are drawn. I can't tell whether the chink of light is natural or emanating from the lamppost that the council in their infinite wisdom chose to erect outside my bedroom window. There are no sounds from the living room. It must be night-time. I don't think they have pitched camp or dared to use one of my guest bedrooms. I am alone. I feel the desperate need to urinate. Is this what it's come to? I used to hire and fire people. Now I am reduced to wearing an adult nappy.

I am woken by a knock at the bedroom door. At least somebody is showing me some courtesy. I'm half expecting to see a priest on the lookout for a deathbed conversion. You're out of luck, if that's the case. But it's a new face to me. He walks towards me with a thermometer. He doesn't even try to engage me. I am a sack of flesh to him. The glass stick under my tongue almost makes me choke. Surely he must notice my eyes are watering but he is too busy writing notes onto the clipboard of papers at my bedside. He leaves the door ajar so that I am privy to the background chatter of daytime television. My acutely and oddly enhanced hearing picks up the asinine remarks of this new charmless character and his partner in crime. I wonder if they work in pairs because I am such a threat. In my present state I must be as dangerous as a rice pudding. I hear him say, "It's probably my last day here today by the look of things." What a prognosis! Was my thermometer reading so bad? I feel no worse than yesterday but perhaps the pills are propping me up.

"Shouldn't one of us measure him to check it's the right size?" They argue over who should commit this unenviable task. Apparently I'm a miserable old sod and neither wants to come into my room unless absolutely necessary. Is my fragile mortality infectious?

"I'll be glad to see the back of him. None of us will shed a tear when he's gone."

They're clearly fitting me up for a coffin.

*****

My afternoon is nap is disturbed by a commotion.

"They're here."

Is this it then? The hearse must be here. I expect it's stopping my neighbours in their tracks. I must be having an out of body experience. Contrary to the views of my family, I must possess a soul after all.

"Should we wash him?"

"No, we can let them do it when they get him there. It's all part of the service." Whoever spoke these words laughed maliciously.

So this is it; no tunnel beckoning me towards the light and definitely no host of cherubs to help me on my journey. The door is opened and a paramedic enters. She speaks gruffly but directly to me. Poor thing, I feel quite sorry for this one. Maybe this is her way of dealing with a corpse. By talking to me, perhaps she is able to humanise me. I wish they'd done this when I'd been alive. She rambles on about measurements and size. I thought that the most important thing about a coffin would be that it is sufficiently capacious to contain all of my body. I don't want to have a stray limb sticking out when they hammer down the lid. Surely it can't ever be too big. Just a waste of wood. I'm not a child with a new pair of shoes. I don't need growing room. She's apparently worried about my posture and comfort. Too late for that now.

"I'll be back in a minute with it." Sweet of her to keep me informed with her running commentary on her actions and intentions; but rather redundant. I couldn't speak after the stroke when I was alive so she's definitely not going to get a response now that I've fallen off my perch. I hope somebody is going to assist her. Even though she's stockily built, there's no way she can manage a coffin single-handedly, especially on the way down with me in it.

She comes back with a wheel chair. Well I never saw this coming. Perhaps she figured that I would still be malleable enough to be placed in it before rigor mortis set in. I can't remember now from all those forensic crime programmes how long it takes. It can't be long. She'd better get a move on. She patiently explains to me that she's going to ask her colleague to help her lift me into the wheelchair and then together they will lift the chair down the stairs and then into the ambulance. I find it rather ironic that only in death is my body accorded any respect.

But instead of leaving, she kneels by my bedside. She strokes my hair and looks straight at me.

"You have been told what's going on, haven't you?"

I am unable to respond but she carries on.

"You've had a nasty stroke that left you greatly paralysed. You've needed rest but the good news is that all the tests show that you could

41

respond to intensive therapy at a rehabilitation centre. We're here to transfer you. There's nothing to be scared about. Doctors can do wonderful things nowadays. There was a hold up ordering the correct sized wheelchair for you."

I open my mouth to say thank you but before I can emit a strangulated sound, she tells me to conserve my energy.

I'll have to wait to find out what it's like to die another time.

Strawberry Fool

Stephen lets me do some of the gardening. It's all first names here. I have my own beds. They help me out with the big bags of compost. As long as I show him my receipts they let me buy whatever plants I want. My favourites are peonies. They remind me of her.

I arrive at half past eight in the morning every Monday, Wednesday and Friday. I take a break for my elevenses and then I pack up at a quarter to one. I'm home for the one o'clock news. When Stephen arrives he always salutes me. Must think I'd been a military man. I never bothered to correct him. I was never called up on account of the accident.

It's pretty miserable weather today. They'd let me inside to have my tea and digestives I'm sure. The woman on reception has even offered in the past. But as I said to her, a little rain never did anyone any harm. She laughed and said as long as you weren't the wicked Witch of the West. She's a card that one. I'm happy perching on the upturned wheel-barrow. She shouts out the window, "We'll have to get you a fishing rod and a gnome's hat." I smile. I told you she was funny.

The joints are playing up today. Mustn't grumble. At eighty-seven I'm only too pleased to be alive. Many of the residents here are younger than me. It's the wet weather. Sets off my rheumatism. I know many people think Autumn is a depressing time of year. I just see it as Mother Nature recharging her batteries.

I'd go conkering as a lad. I had one that just kept on winning. I must have won twenty matches with it. Then it started to crack. That was the year her family moved into the village. There were three daughters but I'd only eyes for Ellen.

Her family caused quite a stir. Their father liked his drink and was arrested a couple of times. Never seemed to be able to hold down a job. Their mother took in mending and washing and somehow kept food on the table for them. We only had two classes at our school. A husband and wife ran it in those days. She was in charge of the little ones where they just played and he taught the other class and tried to prepare us for secondary school. The male teacher gave extra lessons and homework to the ones he reckoned had a chance of getting into the grammar school. They didn't bother with me. I was bigger than all the others, even the older ones. He'd get me moving furniture and when he spotted I had a talent for growing things he let me weed the school gardens. That was until my mother found out. She marched me down to the school and tore a strip off him. I can still remember now her voice as she said at him, "I send my Thomas to school so that you can knock some sense into him. God knows I've tried. He's a kind soul but God never doled out his share of brains. If I wanted him to pull up dandelions I've plenty at home on the farm." She feared nobody. From that day the teacher tried extra hard with me but for some reason the letters made no sense to me. They were all a jumble to my eyes.

Ellen was smart. When she joined our class the teacher never had hard enough books for her. Her sisters were clever too, but she was the brightest. Even I could tell that. She finished everything he set her. She'd wait by his desk while he marked her sums. She never got one wrong. My numbers book was like a one sided game of noughts and crosses.

He used to give her jobs to do in the classroom. Ellen picked some peonies out of somebody's front garden and gave them to the teacher on his birthday. He blushed. She would count the dinner money and if he ever needed a messenger she was asked. I was struggling with my work one morning and he told Ellen to sit with me.

"Can't you do this? A big lad like you!"

I blushed.

"I could do this when I was four. How old are you? Twelve, thirteen? Have they kept you back because you're simple?"

"I'm nine. Just big for my age."

"What does your mother feed you? Whatever it is, it does the trick." I loved the way she laughed, even if it was at my expense.

I couldn't follow when she explained how to do the sums. In the end she just told me the answers. It was strange to see ticks in my book the next day.

I didn't dare approach her at playtimes. Ellen was never alone. It made me happy just to see her. I didn't need to speak with her. Besides, what would I say?

I was surprised one morning, just before lining up to go into class, one of her sisters passed me a note. I could just about make out the few words. I couldn't believe my good fortune. Ellen wanted to meet me in the woods after school.

She seemed to ignore me all day long. Whenever I looked across at her, she turned away. Maybe she was shy after all. I didn't mind because I would have her all to myself that afternoon. I would tell my mother I'd been kept back after school to repeat my work. That had happened plenty of times before.

I thought she'd wait for me when the school bell was rung, but she rushed off. I was excited about finally being alone with her. I knew the part of the woods she meant. There was a rope swing over a little stream. When I reached the spot, I was disappointed to see that she was not alone. Her sisters were whispering to her and there were quite a few other children from our class. Lots of them were grinning. I didn't know exactly who else was there. My mother pressed me for details later, but I only focused on Ellen.

Ellen came towards me with a red scarf. "We're going to play a little game, Thomas."

I don't really remember much. She was egged on by the others. They were shouting and cheering. The wool felt scratchy over my eyes. She took me by the hand and then left me standing. She called me to follow her. Her voice seemed to be coming from all sorts of different directions. She must have climbed a tree as I could hear her calling from above my head. She wanted me to follow her so I began to scale the tree. I recalled the shape of it well and the location of the lowest branches. The others started shouting, "Higher, higher!" I must have been near the top. The last thing I heard from her was, "Over here" before the branch snapped and I fell.

The doctor told my mother I was lucky to be alive. My mother had a load of questions for me. She wanted to know who had done this to me, who had been there in the woods and whose idea was the blindfold. She had her suspicions but I never betrayed Ellen. I just told her I was playing with the other children. I was off school for months. My mother nursed me but couldn't seem to help mentioning all the extra work my accident had caused her. One day she came into my room and announced "You've got a visitor." I knew she wasn't impressed.

I turned and saw Ellen standing near the window. The light was streaming through and seemed to make an orange halo around her abundant red hair. I thought an angel had visited my bedroom. She had a brown paper bag with a few pink stains from the contents inside.

"I picked these for you. I'll fetch more if you like them."

I recognised the strawberry smell. I didn't like them. I pretended I did because she'd done something kind for me. My mother hovered about on the landing. Ellen sat down on the chair next to my bed. She looked around the room.

"You're lucky to have your own room."

My mother couldn't resist adding, "But not so lucky to have both his legs broken. The surgeon said they might never be straight again."

There was a long silence. I thought that Ellen might take this as her cue to leave but she carried on, "Everybody misses you at school. When will you be coming back?"

"The doctor says I might be back in the Autumn."

My mother couldn't resist butting in again, "And missing out on the harvest work! August is our busiest month. I don't know how I'm going to cope."

"My father could help if you need a farmhand," Ellen offered.

My mother just grunted and went downstairs.

Ellen leaned forwards and told me she had some news to tell me.

"My parents have just had a letter. I've won a scholarship to St Agnes. It's a school a long way away. I'll be a boarder."

I'd never heard of St Agnes before but whoever she was, I hated her. I couldn't even pretend to be happy for Ellen. I told her a lie and said I wasn't feeling well. The doctor had only said the previous day that I was making good progress but now I had a sickness in my stomach. I turned over in my bed towards the wall with my back to her. I was worried I might start crying and she'd tell everyone I was a baby.

She stood up to go. "I thought you'd be happy for me."

"I am," I mumbled, without turning towards her.

She must have been standing there for a couple of minutes. I'd hoped she'd left. I turned over in the bed and she was still there, standing in the doorway. She looked down at the floor and muttered, "I'm sorry about your legs."

That was it. She never came to see me again.

I went back to the school in September and had crutches for a while but I soon worked out how to get by without them. Ellen only came back in the holidays and then a few years later her family moved away from the village. Her dad had left for good and Ellen's mother took her daughters to live nearer her own mother. I heard all this from my mother. I feigned a lack of interest but inside I was desperate to hear anything about her.

By the time the war started I was ready to leave school. There was no way that my services would ever be called upon. I did learn to walk independently but I always had a pronounced limp. I got used to it. I spent the war years driving a bus. I heard about Ellen from time to time. She married and had a family. That's what my mother told me.

"She was the only girl you were ever soft on. You can't trust people with ginger hair. She would've led you a merry dance."

I wanted to leap to Ellen's defence and explain her hair was strawberry blonde and that she was kind deep down. But I didn't bother. There was no point disagreeing with my mother. Once she had an idea fixed in her head there was no budging it. She always had it in for Ellen and her family as soon as they moved into the village, always criticising their clothes or the way they spoke or the fact that her mother didn't keep the front step clean.

My mother was right about one thing though, there was never anyone else I was sweet on. It's daft really. I'm not saying I've lived a life of a monk; I've had several lady friends over the years. It's just that there was nobody who made me feel the way she did. I didn't want to settle for second best.

*****

I've finished for the morning now. I just need to wash down my tools and sweep up. Here's a car I don't recognise. I know all the vehicles of the staff and regular visitors. This one is pretty full. Maybe it's a new resident. There was a death last week and they've had the decorators in smartening up the room. Yes, I was right, there's an elderly woman in the passenger seat. Must be her daughter bringing all the belongings through. You'd think she'd attend to her own mother first. She opens the passenger door and releases her mother from her seat belt. The elderly woman simply sits and stares out in front of her. Several members of staff come out to assist and I overhear the daughter telling them about her mother over the old woman's head. The words 'dementia' and 'stroke' sit in the air. They lift the woman into a wheelchair. You'd think that one of them would have given her a blanket to cover her legs. It's turned chilly. As they pass me, the woman turns to face me. It can't be her. The hair is white. But the smile is the same.

*****

The receptionist was surprised to see me back at the nursing home that afternoon.

"Doing some overtime, Thomas?"

I hardly noticed what she said to me. I just wanted to see Ellen again. I smiled.

"I would like to visit somebody. There was a lady who came in at lunchtime. I think I know her."

The receptionist joked about me being a dark horse and whether I needed a chaperone.

Ellen's room was on the first floor. I took the lift. As I waited for the doors to close I took a proper look in the mirror and checked my tie was straight. My mother had a put down for all occasion. Today's would have been, 'There's no fool like an old fool'.

Ellen was lying in her bed. The journey must have exhausted her. I could see her fine hair spread out on her pillow as her eyes were facing the ceiling. I knocked on the door. There was an orderly putting her clothes away. She must have been from an agency as she didn't recognise me. She simply said that she would leave us alone. She must have thought I was her husband. I did have a bunch of flowers in my hand. She took the flowers from me, saying she would put the peonies in water. I hovered in the doorway.

Eventually I plucked up the courage to go in. Ellen did not turn her face to me. I sat myself down in the chair by the window. The orderly came back with the flowers in a vase and placed them on the windowsill.

I must have been sitting there for ages. Perhaps I nodded off. All of a sudden the orderly reappeared, "You're still here? We're a bit short staffed. Would you mind feeding your wife?"

I didn't bother to correct her. I simply agreed. I helped her sit Ellen up in bed and adjusted the table so that it was in front of her. The orderly placed the unappetising supper on the table. It was beginning to get dark outside. I fastened the bib around Ellen's neck and managed to feed her a few mouthfuls of the nondescript meal. She simply refused to eat anymore. She kept her mouth shut and shook her head. I fantasised about the sort of meal I could have prepared for her at home. I'd become quite a good cook over the years. I placed the tray on her bedside table. I just began talking about the past. I didn't know how much she understood or even heard but it made me feel better. I listed my precious memories; the smell of the blackboard when it was newly repainted at the beginning of each term, the excitement of being given a new exercise book and the day our teacher was sick so we were sent home early. But the best of all was the day she came to my school.

The orderly returned with the dessert. "Maybe she'll like this. The food'll take time to get used to. It says 'strawberry fool' on the menu. Looks like yogurt to me."

As I spoon-fed Ellen the pink pudding a small smile appeared on her face. I wondered whether she remembered the reversal of positions. For me, even after all these years, it was as clear as yesterday when she came to visit and I was in bed with her gift of strawberries.

When she'd finished every last bit I dabbed her face with the paper serviette. I placed the bowl and spoon on the table and moved it away from the bed. I put on my coat and went to leave. I turned to say goodbye one more time and to have one last look. She no longer gazed up above. Instead she looked straight at me. I couldn't hear what she said so I walked slowly towards her and knelt by her bed. My knees creaked as I lowered myself down. I could feel her hot breath on my cheek as I turned my ear to her face. It clearly took her a great effort to whisper, "I'm so sorry about your legs."

Waste Not, Want Not

They placed it there overnight. When I drew my curtains one morning, it was there. The black, squat monstrosity was situated on the street directly in front of our building, obscuring my view and virtually blocking all daylight to my basement flat. I calmed myself by saying it may be a temporary measure. As I ate my breakfast, the radio could not drown out the noise from outside. Every couple of minutes a person would deposit their rubbish into the container and the lid would be slammed down. Intolerable!

If they hadn't been short staffed in the shop I would have gone up to the council office that very morning. I would have demanded to meet the moron whose brainwave it had been and explain how its continued presence would blight my life. But Kylie was up at the hospital and Stewart was on holiday so I had to open up the shop. I satisfied myself by leaving a message on the voicemail of the refuse disposal department. Nobody would probably hear it but it made me feel better.

*****

That was a few weeks ago. My black metallic nemesis remains parked outside. Surely local people do not possess this obscene amount of rubbish? We must be attracting bin bags from neighbouring streets. I reckon we must be listed on some obscure website that attracts bin-spotters from out of town. Maybe they make a day trip out of it, simply to deposit their waste in a receptacle right outside my home. I was worried that the rubbish would overflow and clog up the pavement. But in this respect the local council is uncharacteristically efficient. They come and empty the container as soon as it is full, regardless of the time seemingly; day or night. It makes a terrible racket as it is upturned and its contents are dropped into a refuse lorry where the bags are crushed. I was pretty impressed the first time that I saw this happen but now I am plagued by the noise it makes and the disruption to my peaceful existence. Deep breaths. The doctor warned me about this. Must remain calm when they arrive. I'm unsure why they have to travel in pairs but when I finally managed to arrange a meeting with representatives of the council, two councillors were promised. Is that a brace or is that just for grouse?

They should be arriving in about fifteen minutes. I've laid out a tray with biscuits. I found three matching cups and saucers. I hope they don't mind instant coffee. I've written a list of my grievances. Number one is obvious. Why the hell did they park that thing there? I further object to the notice that has now appeared on the side of the bin. No doubt it is the outcome of some health and safety think tank. It has the image of a stick figured man climbing into the bin with a huge black cross superimposed. Just to hammer the point home the wording next to it defies belief. Readers are warned not to climb into the bin as it may be dangerous. Good grief! Any imbecile who decides to spend the night in one of those things deserves what fate has in store for them at the local tip.

There is a ring at the doorbell. As I open the door I come face to face with somebody who can be no older than fourteen.

"Good morning. Sorry if I'm a little late." He checks his wristwatch. I half expect it to have Mickey Mouse on it as a recent birthday present from his mum and dad. "Five minutes late, please forgive me. I'm afraid my colleague is unable to come today. So it's just me. Shall I come in?"

He thrusts out his hand to shake. I'm temporarily stunned at the self-confidence of such a young person. Has he started shaving yet?

"Yes of course, just through here."

I sense his eyes scanning the room for tell-tale signs of my political leanings or interests. I'd stashed away my TV guides and the book I'm currently reading – a little low-brow. He sits in my best arm chair and I perch on the sofa. This is not what I'd intended. The seating plan has been reversed. He politely declines my offer of refreshments. He seems to read my mind.

"I know. I do look rather young. Some of my constituents expect to see me in a school blazer. The age restriction was lowered for councillors a few years back. I'd just turned eighteen and the papers made quite a thing of it when I won the election. Even got a *Guinness Book of Records* mention. Only a council position but perhaps the gateway for future glory. Ten Downing Street one day." He then laughed at his pitiful excuse for a joke. I hate it when people do that. I vaguely recalled the media fuss about him but I was certainly not going to give him the satisfaction of recognition.

"So what are you going to do about that eyesore?"

"Well I certainly appreciate your forthright approach. Too many people in politics like the sounds of their own voices and skirt around—"

"When can you get it moved?"

He clearly wasn't accustomed to interruptions. He loosened his tie and smiled at me in a most unconvincing fashion.

"Well I do need to make a confession to you."

This was not the approach I had been expecting. There was a dramatic pause. Was he about to unburden himself?

"The council's new refuse collection system is my baby. I introduced a streamlined means of—"

"Are you trying to tell me that you are the person responsible for that hideous carbuncle outside?"

"Well, all councillors of the ruling party technically share a collective responsibility for all decisions taken and I feel I must point out how ground-breaking our exciting new initiative is. It has eliminated the need for dustbins and wheelchair access along narrow pavements has been greatly enhanced. Obviously there was a considerable outlay at the outset of this scheme, but within three years we hope to be making savings in the region of..."

I let him carry on. He gleefully rattled off figures extolling the virtues of 'his baby'. How our little authority would be a pilot for this ambitious scheme which could become national or even worldwide. When he finally ran out of steam, he smiled at me again. He clearly thought he'd won me over.

I paused for a few seconds. 'Is it going or not?'

"Well, Miss...or is it Mrs?"

"That's none of your business. Now please answer my question." I waved my hand dismissively for effect. This obviously unsettled him.

"We all live in a community and I see this council ward as an extended family–"

I couldn't stop myself from interrupting. "I have lived in this flat for eleven years. I neither know the names of my neighbours nor have the remotest inclination to find out."

"We have to learn to live together as a community and we can't allow a nimby attitude to pervade–"

"What type of attitude?"

He then went on to smugly explain that it stood for not in my back yard. What a truly hideous acronym! I pretended that I knew what it stood for and that my look of incomprehension was due to the fact that he was daring to pursue his argument.

"And another thing, why on earth do you place those ridiculous warning posters on the side of the bins? Could they not be stuck on the other side facing the street so I don't have to see it every time I leave my home?"

"Our health and safety executive have advised us that in the light of the tragic accident, whereby a rather inebriated soul intended to spend the night in one of our refuse containers–"

"You mean that some fool actually climbed into one and was crushed to death?"

"Yes, unfortunately so. That is why the warning signs have to be clearly visible."

"He deserved it. Bloody idiot, it serves him right!"

"If you don't mind me saying, that's not terribly public spirited of you."

After an awkward silence, he requested a glass of water. I obliged. He attempted to change the topic of conversation to more neutral subjects. Within a couple of minutes he had discovered that 'yes' it was warm for the time of year, 'no' I was not going away on holiday this summer and that I would not under any circumstances be voting for him or his party.

*****

I'm in a mess. I've taken one of my tablets. I'm using the brown paper bag the nurse suggested for hyperventilation. My breathing is gradually returning to normal. I just need to sit quietly. It was never going to be an easy meeting. I detested his smarminess. The minimum I expected was for him to offer some sort of reconsideration. Perhaps they would agree to a rotational system whereby the bin is not permanently parked outside our building. But no, I could see that I would be saddled with this for eternity and that he was proud of his 'initiative'. I think his comment about me not being public spirited was the trigger. I couldn't help myself.

Tiny beads of sweat had begun to appear on his forehead. He'd asked me for an aspirin. He really didn't look at all well. When I'd come back from the kitchen with the electric carving knife and a roll of heavy duty bin bags he just looked at me like a little puppy. By this time the large dose of ketamine in his glass of water had taken effect. His central nervous system had been shot to bits. I may not be a fully trained pharmacist but working in the chemist shop all these years had taught me a few things.

At least I won't have to worry about the disposal of his body. I only had to use three bags. They won't lie around on the street for days. Pretty impressive refuse collection really when you think about it.

Dangerous Precedent

Doreen started five months ago in the charity shop. She wanted to work for a good cause. She had dismissed the ones for animals or foreign orphans immediately; she would let others care for them. The lady at the NSPCC had been friendly but there had been no volunteer vacancies. So Doreen found herself at Mind. She counted herself lucky that no-one in her family had been touched by mental illness. It must be dreadful she concluded, after reading some of the leaflets they had displayed at the till.

She had not started 'front of house' but instead spent her first six weeks as one of Susan's 'backroom gals'. This involved rummaging through the bags of donated goods, which were mostly left, out of hours, outside the shop. This was despite the increasingly blunt signs that Susan put up in the window to discourage this particular practice. A large amount of the contents could be binned immediately, especially if the bags had not been tied securely and it had been raining. Doreen found it difficult to fathom what possessed people to donate underwear with holes or stains. The washing machine was in almost constant use. She was content when she was on ironing duty. It had been a long time since she needed to press a week's worth of work shirts for the two men in her life.

This morning, Doreen arrives a full half hour before trading officially begins. She has to wait in the shop doorway for Susan – 'Call me Sue, everyone does' – to arrive. She is one of the designated keyholders; perhaps some day, Doreen might become one too. She believes in punctuality, or rather is driven by the dread of being late. Besides, she wants to impress Susan and thus retain her hard-earned position on the shop floor. As Susan fiddles about with the alarm code, Doreen makes the first tea of the day.

Margaret cuts it fine, as usual. She seems to have a fresh excuse every Wednesday, which is her only day in the shop. Doreen has built up to two and a half days. After all, she has plenty of time on her hands now.

The three of them gather in the small office for the daily 'team meeting'. Doreen can never read upside down what is written on Susan's clipboard. Margaret clearly thinks it to be a complete waste of time and examines her nails thoroughly. The tasks assigned are similar and repetitive but Doreen listens attentively for the next 'bullet point'.

It is only half past ten and there are no customers in the shop. Business is very slow this morning. This provides Doreen ample opportunity to ensure that the books are in alphabetical order by author. This activity provides a large amount of pleasure for her. They need a shelf just for the letter C: Jackie Collins, Agatha Christie and Catherine Cookson are terribly popular. Her tea is undrinkable. She won't make a fuss though; doesn't want to upset Margaret. Doreen is very particular about her sugar intake nowadays. She has cut down to a half a teaspoon. But this mug contains at least one spoonful, and heaped at that. She has told her fellow volunteer on countless occasions but it never seems to go in. At home she serves herself with a cup and saucer but here she is grateful for anything without a chip. She will wait until nobody is looking and pour it down the sink. What a waste.

As she turns off the tap, Doreen catches her reflection. It must have been vanity that caused Margaret to salvage this antique effect mirror. She, no doubt, hung it above the sink, so she can check on her make-up every time she fills the kettle or rinses out a cup. A few weeks ago, Margaret let slip a detail which betrayed her age and Doreen had almost been shocked, at least certainly a little surprised. Margaret was eleven years older but from their appearances the reverse could be nearer the truth. Doreen can see what her sister means now, when she sends her money off vouchers for anti-ageing cream. Visiting the hairdresser is a luxury she had foregone several years ago. After all, the legal bills were crippling.

Susan stands behind her and says, "Not like you, Doreen to be skulking out here, daydreaming. I need you out front. There's a bit of a rush on. Chop, chop. Where's Margaret? In the loo?"

Doreen objects to that word but lets it pass without wincing. She nods, even though she knows Margaret has popped out the back for a cigarette.

As Doreen emerges through the plastic beaded curtain back into the shop, she observes Susan in hard sell mode. A middle-aged man has shown interest in a tea service in the window. Susan is busy extolling its mint condition in order to justify its £45 price tag. There is a young woman looking at the scarves. So Doreen positions herself behind the counter, as a purchase seems imminent.

"How much is this one?"

"They're all £1.25. The sign must have fallen down again." Doreen is just being polite as she can see the sign in its rightful place from behind the till. The young woman looks in the different compartments of her purse and then starts going through all of her pockets.

"Not got enough, dear? Show us how much you've got."

The young woman wordlessly shows Doreen the handful of coins. They count them out together on the counter. She is 30p short.

"Not to worry, that'll be enough."

Doreen hears her name called. "Excuse me a minute, dear. My supervisor needs me."

Doreen follows Susan into the changing cubicle. Susan pulls the makeshift curtain behind them. "What are you doing, Doreen? You do not have the authority to discount items."

"I thought that I was doing the right thing. We've had that scarf for over two months and finally we're selling it. Besides, she looks like a student and probably can't afford much."

"It is not up to you to make those types of decisions."

Doreen can feel her face reddening. "But what can I do now? I've already said…"

"Too much," Susan interrupted.

"I know…I'll put thirty pence in the till out of my own money, that way we'll be alright."

This suggestion seems to infuriate Susan even further. "Do you realise what that would do? It would set a dangerous precedent and we would have every student and down and out haggling over every item. This may be a charity shop, Doreen, but we are not in the business of dispensing charity. We have our targets to reach. Now, go and inform her that you have made a mistake."

"May I put it to one side, if she would like to come back later with the correct money?"

"On this occasion, yes. But if unsold, it goes back on sale tomorrow morning."

It is humiliating having to explain to the young woman. They are both embarrassed about the situation. Susan stares and is not satisfied until she witnesses the young woman leaving the shop without the scarf. Margaret reappears at this time, reeking of polo mints. "Anyone fancy a drink?"

Susan and Doreen both decline the offer.

After a few minutes, Doreen goes out the back to look for a duster and some polish. She never likes to be idle. She interrupts Margaret touching up her coral pink lipstick.

"Has she been laying the law down again?"

"It's nothing, really. I just wanted to be kind to that young woman. That's all. She reminded me of someone."

"Well, don't let Susan get you down. We're working for nothing here. She can't treat you like a skivvy, don't forget that; especially not in front of the customers."

While Margaret is talking and recounting Susan's faults, Doreen remembers. The young woman reminded her of a neighbour's daughter. Stephen went out with her a few times. But it hadn't worked out. Her son had not shown sufficient interest. It just fizzled out. There hadn't been many girlfriends. He seemed happier alone in his room.

"Don't you agree, Doreen?"

She chooses a diplomatic nod, which seems to pacify Margaret.

*****

Doreen never takes all of her forty-five minute lunch break. She is always back within half an hour. She eats her homemade sandwiches on a bench by the bandstand if it is fine. But today, the grey drizzle means she is confined to the bus station. She is never tempted by the shops. When she downsized from a semi-detached house to a one bedroom flat, her problem had been finding space for things she chose to keep. Her husband only lasted six months in the flat. He pined for his garden. She had made enquiries to the council about an allotment but the waiting list was over a year. If the registrar had been accurate on the certificate, shame would have been the cause of death.

"Boo!" wheezes Margaret, cigarette in hand, "You look miles away."

"Sorry, I was."

"Down memory lane? Fancy coming for a coffee before we get back to the shop? She sent me for lunch early. Said she'd manage on her own; what a trouper, shall we give her a medal? It will be good to have a gossip with you. What's the worst she can do? Sack us?"

"No, I'd best be heading back. Susan's asked me to sort through the ties and match them with the shirts. It's a new idea she's had about showing customers..."

"Sounds riveting, Doreen. Think I'll leave you to it and grab some more fresh air," she says as she lights a new cigarette from her dying stub.

It is not solely the thought of facing Susan's wrath for tardiness, but the potentially prohibitive price of the hot drink. Doreen knows of some places that charge more than £2.50. That she cannot afford.

*****

"Back nice and early. I can always rely on you, Doreen."

The conciliatory tone from Susan means that a favour is about to be asked.

"I've just been putting the finishing touches to the rotas for next week and was wondering whether you could work next Friday? I know that's not your regular day."

"I'm sorry I can't. I have something arranged."

"Can't you change it, Doreen?"

Susan explains in a convoluted and increasingly desperate fashion how she is short staffed on that particular day. This involves planned holidays and unexpected hospital appointments.

"It would help us out so much."

"I'm sorry, Susan, but I am unable to help out on this occasion."

"Are you quite sure? I really need..."

"No."

Susan is temporarily silenced by Doreen's assertive tone.

The remainder of the day passes with scant conversation between the two of them. Margaret attempts unsuccessfully to prise out of Doreen the cause of the atmosphere in the shop but she is not forthcoming with any details. Margaret offers to make tea at twenty minute intervals but her beverage interventions are rebuffed by both Susan and Doreen.

Susan turns the open sign to closed and her volunteers go to collect their coats.

"If you have a minute please, Doreen, I would like a quick word with you, once I've finished cashing up."

Margaret hesitates.

"You go ahead, Margaret. I'll catch you up and if the bus comes you get it."

"No, I'll wait out the back, Doreen, I'm not in a..."

"This shouldn't take long, but we would appreciate some privacy, Margaret."

She walks to the door and pulls a face behind Susan's back. She mouths a "phone me later" to Doreen.

Once they are alone in the shop, Susan turns away from Doreen and clears her throat. There is a pause.

"I'm disappointed in you, Doreen."

"If it's about the scarf, Susan..."

"No, it's not just that, but it does demonstrate that you may not be suited to this type of work; not everyone is. It takes a special sort of person to work here. It's not as easy as it looks."

"Is it about next Friday?"

"No. Again, that just showed me that I have to question your commitment to the organisation. I, myself, have sacrificed several important appointments for the sake of the charity. After all, that's the reason we're here. I am beginning to feel that you do not place a large enough priority on the work that we do here."

Doreen all but bites her tongue. She is sorely tempted to point out that the significant difference between them is that Susan is a paid employee and that she is a volunteer.

"I'm being swamped by volunteer applicants and I am having to review our current staffing arrangements. I am going to have to consider your position here very carefully."

"So what does that mean for me, Susan? Don't you want me to work here anymore?"

"I think that would be best for everyone. I would be willing to waive any notice period under these circumstances. It would be easier and less embarrassing for you if you send me a letter of resignation. Head office like that sort of thing for their records. Keep it nice and simple. I always try to keep them happy. That way, nobody, except us, would ever need to know that you had been let go."

"Please, Susan, give me another chance. I have nothing else."

"Don't make this any more awkward than it needs to be. This is much harder for me..."

"Isn't there anything I can do to make you change your mind?"

Susan rearranges a collection of glass figurines and without looking up at Doreen says, "Well, perhaps if you were able to work next Friday I might reconsider. I'm too forgiving a person. It's one of my greatest faults."

*****

On her way home, Doreen worries about the call she will have to make. As she lets herself in through the front door the phone is ringing. She is certain that it will be Margaret, wanting to know what had happened. Besides, nobody else calls her these days, unless they are selling something. The journalists stopped calling; moved on years ago to newer stories. Margaret can wait until tomorrow.

Doreen looks through her drawer of important papers. She finds a recent letter which gives her a list of visiting dates. For a split second she hopes that she is mistaken. Perhaps it isn't next Friday. Maybe she had got it wrong. No, the date leaps off the page at her. She feels sick that she has betrayed her son for Susan. Everyone else had given up on Stephen, and now she has joined their ranks. She dials the number under the address at the top of the page and gives the extension number to the operator.

She feels terrible enough about relinquishing a precious opportunity to visit her only child. In his letters Stephen says that her visits are the only thing keeping him going. This is a new development. One of the prison hospital doctors told her this is a good sign. Her son is 'working through his anger'. She did not understand the phrase fully. She is simply relieved that he has not blamed her for several months now. Maybe the new drugs are working after all. Her husband called their own flesh and blood a monster. He sided with the press.

She does not recognise the voice. It must be a new member of staff in the high security wing. Doreen is spoken to as if she is a novice to visiting arrangements. This newcomer points out to Doreen over the crackly telephone line how important routine is to her son's recovery.

Doreen hears how any disappointment could have a profoundly detrimental effect on Stephen. It may not be possible to arrange another visit for the following week. She meekly says that she understands and apologises profusely. Doreen is informed that she will receive a revised visiting schedule and that she must view keeping the allotted appointment as a high priority. This is the second person today who has questioned her priorities. Who could have done more for their son? She had given up so much for him; selling her home, losing her husband, the futile legal appeals.

Doreen sits in front of the television with the volume turned down. Her cup of tea has just the right level of sweetness. One of the newsreaders reminds her of her son's victim; so many women do these days. Doreen works out how old she would have been.

Out of the Blue

I'll give my wife another five minutes. Maybe she got chatting to somebody. It's not likely though. It's cold out and we both want to get to bed.

It's now 11:30 p.m. and she's been out with the dog for half an hour. She hates it when I worry about her. 'I'm an independent woman,' she says frequently. I've emptied the dishwasher and cleaned the kitchen surfaces. I'd ring her mobile but she'd hate that. 'Stop fussing!' she often says.

It's almost midnight and I've rearranged everything in the fridge. It's amazing how untidy it gets. She doesn't help though. I'm sure she hides things at the back so they go well past their sell by date. I can't bear waste.

It's no good. I'm going to call her. She won't like it. It'll probably start off a tirade about patriarchal oppression but I'm seriously worried now. There's no answer. It goes to voicemail.

I've still got the ironing board up. I'll finish off a few things to take my mind off her. That way, when she comes back I can act all natural. There are a few scrunched up tee-shirts that need an iron. There's the funny one she was wearing the night we met almost ten years ago. The caption made me laugh. It still does. *A woman needs a man like a goldfish needs a bicycle.*

I plump up the sofa cushions while I wait for the iron to cool down. She's left the Sunday newspaper sections lying all over the place. I fold them properly and place them in the rack. There's an advert for a toy store on the back of one of the supplements. Makes me wonder why we never got around to having children. When I bring up the subject, she always says, 'What if it's a boy?' I smile at her little joke. She doesn't. I love her deadpan humour.

At least the dog will be having a good walk. She wasn't my first choice at the animal rescue centre. But I've grown to love her. I wanted the Labrador. He wasn't much more than a puppy. He was so playful and had loads of energy. She said, 'I'm not having another penis in the house. I can smell the testosterone from here.' I told you she was funny. That's why we ended up with Saffy. That's what I call her anyway. She's named after a Greek poet. She gets cross when I call Sappho a poetess. Says that's sexist. I don't understand why. I bought Saffy a lovely blue collar when we first had her. My wife threw it away. Apparently blue is a masculine colour. I do think my wife has some strange ideas at times.

It's no good. I'm going to have to go and look for her. 'I can look after myself,' she's always pointing out to me. 'Why do you think I run those self-defence classes at the women's centre?' Once, I suggested that it was probably to get a break from me. She never laughs at my jokes.

I have to check that the four gas rings are off. I haven't even used the cooker tonight but it's become a habit. Just like the hand washing. I like my little routines. They make me feel safe. I just need to pop upstairs to make sure I haven't left the bathroom tap running. I know I haven't been up there this evening but it's good to be on the safe side.

As I zip up my fleece, I walk towards the small patch of grass at the end of our road. I can see her in the distance. Yes, it is her and Saffy. I can see their silhouettes. But she's leaning forward and talking to somebody in a car. I expect she's giving them directions. My Good Samaritan. I stop and watch. I'm waiting for her to notice me. I'm fifty yards away. I can't believe it. She's opening the car door and putting Saffy in the back. Then she gets in the car herself in the front seat. She knows better than to get into a stranger's car. She's always telling me about the proliferation of predatory kerb-crawling males. I run as fast as I can before the car speeds off.

I call the police and I tell them that she's been abducted. I'm worried I'll forget the number plate that I've memorised as they keep asking me questions. I blurt out the letter and numbers. The kind woman on the other end of the phone asks whether the car could belong to a friend. Of course it can't be a friend. I apologise for shouting to her. She promises that they will run the number plate through their database. I remind her that the first few hours after a disappearance are the vital ones and they need to post her details to all ferry ports and airports. The police officer reassures me that they will do all that they can but that in most cases the missing person turns ups safely. She asks whether we have had an argument. I resent the intrusion into my private life but I know that they are just doing their duty. "Things couldn't be better," I reply. She informs me that I need to call back in the morning if she hasn't returned. I can't believe that the police are not offering to do more.

*****

I've hardly slept. It's not really surprising. I must have dozed for a bit I suppose because it's almost light. There's been no word of her. I make myself a mug of tea. I almost trip over Saffy's bowl. I can't believe they're both gone: kidnapped and dognapped. The policewoman had told me to wait for twelve hours before I call back. The hands of the kitchen clock seem to have stopped. I try to distract myself with housework but it seems pointless without her. She's the reason I make our home so perfect.

I call at midday and am told that the car belongs to Ms Dawn Kirby. "That can't be right," I say. "She's a friend of ours. My wife met her on a women's retreat last year in Lesbos. She's been to our house lots of times."

I'm in shock. I notice that many of her clothes are missing and so is her suitcase. She hasn't taken any photographs of me. They're all present and correct but she has taken the ones of her and Saffy. Then I spot an envelope by the side of her bed. She doesn't usually allow me into her bedroom. We have separate rooms as she said she couldn't cope with my snoring. I don't mind the single bed in the box-room.

I can't believe what I'm reading. She claims that we're just not compatible and that she's gone to start a new life with Dawn. My wife has run off with another woman. I don't know what I'll tell our friends.

I won't blame myself, though. It's totally out of the blue. It's not as if there were signs or anything.

Message in a Bottle

My handwriting's crap. So it's word-processed or nothing. It doesn't betray my gender too. If I put smiley faces over my *i*'s then you might think I was a woman. You see, I know all about psychology and how the human brain works. Just because I got written off at school, doesn't mean I'm stupid. I got picked on a lot. The teachers weren't much help. In the end, Mum said I didn't have to go. So I stopped at home. She said she liked the company and I taught myself from books from the library.

I've been reading about E.M. Forster recently. He went on about 'only connecting'. I wish I knew how. They never taught me this at school. I learned about periodic tables and the subjunctive but never about communicating. They call it small talk but to me it's enormous; my North face of the Eiger.

At work my social life consists of the annual Christmas party. It's the highlight of my year but it always disappoints. Every year I hope it'll be different. But it's always the same. I can see them all making excuses to avoid sitting next to me. It can't be that I smell. Mum buys me special soap and I make sure I have an extra long bath that week. I don't bite and I pay for my meal like everyone else. I hear them all laughing at things but they go quiet when I join in.

I got excited once when the boss called an impromptu staff meeting. Everyone looked really miserable. Even though I knew it was about planned redundancies, it gave me the chance to mingle. But I blew it. I kept offering people a bite of my sandwich. Nobody was in the mood for some of my mum's homemade piccalilli. I thought it was a good icebreaker.

I overhear them sometimes in the staff canteen, moaning about appraisals. I look forward to them because it means I get somebody to myself for at least half an hour. Another human being, apart from Mum, has to sit and show interest in me. My last two have been cancelled, it's a shame.

I've tried hobbies. I went to a meeting at a local pub back room for *Dungeons and Dragons* fanatics. I sat nursing my half pint of cider and blackcurrant while they discussed the existence of trolls. They're a bunch of nutters. I didn't go back. I'm better off staying in at home watching television with Mum. She sits in her armchair. It wouldn't seem right somehow for me to use Dad's, so I lie on the sofa. Sometimes she lets me use the remote control.

The car maintenance course could have been great. I have a thirst for knowledge. I could save up for our own car and not worry about the cost if it went wrong. I could always fix it myself. I could take Mum out for trips. She'd like that.

Last September I enrolled. I was so excited about meeting new people, even though they're more likely to be men. I liked all the diagrams around the room on posters in the classroom at the adult education centre. I was in a good mood that evening and plucked up the courage to suggest going for a drink afterwards. The tutor said he was busy and the others didn't say anything. As I walked home alone, I saw a big group of them through the pub window. The tutor was at the bar getting a round in. I was so angry. I couldn't go home. Mum would've asked how it went. So I went for a walk. I ended up along the canal. I don't remember much about it. She was waiting up when I got back. "I was worried about you, son. I didn't know what had happened to you, walking alone at this time of night. It's past midnight. What's that on your hands?"

Then I remembered the cat. I didn't mean to do it.

"I'm tired, Mum," I mumbled as I went up to bed.

I got a refund for the remainder of the term. I had to give a reason on a form for wanting a refund. I wrote that it just wasn't my cup of tea.

I volunteered for the St John's Ambulance. I spent ages on the application form. I must have done a good job because they asked me along to a training day. I didn't know quite what to wear. Mum was convinced that if I was smart, that would impress them. So I wore Dad's old wedding suit. Mum only had to take the trousers up about six inches and I folded back the ends of the sleeves. I fainted at the talk about nosebleeds, even though they only used tomato ketchup on the dummy. They were very kind about it. A lady let me have a lie down and made me a mug of tea. I didn't have the heart to tell her I didn't take sugar. She told me not to worry that not everybody was cut out for this type of thing. I went back for another try when they taught us about fractures. I told everybody about the splints I made for sick animals I found. In the end they wrote me a nice letter thanking me for coming along to some of their training sessions. Funding cuts meant they had to limit the number of places. They promised to let me know if a vacancy came up. Mum put the letter in a scrapbook. They never wrote back.

*****

So this is my seventeenth letter. I always put them in an empty Diet Coke bottle. The first few I dropped off the end of piers when I had daytrips to the seaside. I'd watch them bob around on the waves. I chose Brighton and Southend. I was worried somebody would tell me off for littering. Nothing came of them. Nobody wrote back. Maybe they got washed up in France and they couldn't read English. So now I leave them at different spots in the city. This one I left on a bench outside the library. I have a map on my bedroom wall of all the locations I have positioned them and the date. I don't always write this much. I'm quite chatty today. Thank you for reading this far. My email address is on the back. I place no demands on you. I just don't want to be lonely anymore. You'd be the first to get back to me. That could be a testament to the council's street cleaning service or the realisation that it's true what my father said. Nobody would ever want to be my friend. I shan't repeat the exact words he would scream at me. They were nasty and mean words. He can't say them anymore. My mum put a stop to that. I've a lot to thank her for. Fortunately she's not so squeamish about blood.

Suicide is Painless

The first time I died was in 1997.

It was a rather rushed affair. I saw my window of opportunity at the end of August. Nobody would look too closely into my demise. I'd never been a huge fan of the Royal Family but to this day I appreciate the hoo-ha that surrounded Diana's death. Mother Teresa hardly caused a ripple by dying that week so I would never even register on my own invention – *The Sliding Scale of Death*. Please excuse my gallows humour. This was my own creation. It was to measure the effect that one person's death would have on the national consciousness. I provided a definition running to several paragraphs with impressive looking links but unfortunately Wikipedia declined to include it. I wanted to give Beaufort and Richter some healthy competition. Pity.

I'd left a hurried, incoherent letter in my bedsit. I rambled on for a few pages about how I couldn't go on anymore, nobody loved me, blah, blah, blah – self-indulgent tosh. I thought of finishing it with 'Goodbye cruel world' but I decided against that. I didn't want to overegg the suicidal pudding. I was fortunate with the weather. The currents were particularly strong that evening when I supposedly jumped off Beachy Head. I know it's a cliché but please forgive me. After all, I was a novice at this stage. The coastguards said in the local press that there would be little chance of retrieving my remains, as my body would have been swept out to sea.

My estate consisted of a small insurance policy and precious little else. I had left instructions in my will to dispose of all my belongings to local charities. I bequeathed the money to a long-lost, fictitious, distant cousin in Scotland. When I claimed the payout I think I was rather convincing, even if I say so myself. I chatted to the solicitor's assistant for some time about the loneliness of modern existence and how sad it was that I had not been able to reach out to my deceased relative. My regret at the time was that the death payment was rather modest. Perhaps I should have paid higher monthly premiums. It was a valuable lesson.

I had made few friends in my life. Please, no sympathy. I simply found little use for them. You end up having to care or feel things. Such wasted emotion. But there was the outside possibility that I would bump into a former work colleague, who'd heard I'd died, if I stayed in England. So I settled in France. A short ferry hop and not even a half glance at my new passport at Calais. I needn't have bothered. My money was securely earning me interest in my Swiss bank account. It's a terribly efficient system – I recommend it. I kept some aside for living expenses but that wouldn't last forever.

I had planned to lie low for a while. I reinvented myself as a nondescript borderline simpleton, for whom repetitive factory work was a challenge. I was readily employed by a company manufacturing fireworks. Their health and safety regulations were woefully lax, especially the close proximity of the assigned smoking area to the abundance of combustible materials. I was a firm believer in the adage that when all you have is lemons, lemonade is the most appropriate beverage to concoct. So, surrounded by copious quantities of potassium nitrate and sulphur, the addition of the lit match caused a fantastic pyrotechnic display that illuminated the Toulouse skyline one summer's evening. There was considerable attention in the local press paid to the unfortunate British night-watchman who had tragically been the sole victim of the accidental explosion. Police were not hopeful of finding much or any of his body for burial as he had been at the very epicentre of the blast.

I was on a train to Warsaw the next morning. I would have liked to know how much I would be missed by my colleagues. I travelled across international borders without having to present my paperwork, thanks to the European Union Schengen Treaty. Occasionally I wondered whether my death had inspired a floral tribute at the gates of the factory. But I'm not one for sentimentality so I dismissed such mawkish thoughts.

The insurance company was not terribly prompt in paying. I considered writing a formal complaint to their trustees but decided against it. The sum received this time was quite considerable. I allowed myself a healthy percentage and invested the rest. I became a tourist for a few months. Eastern Europe was refreshingly inexpensive. On one occasion, I could have sworn that I saw my old geography teacher. She was part of one of those guided tour groups which I so assiduously avoided. I realised I wasn't a huge fan of Polish baroque ecclesiastical architecture. I was gazing unimpressed at the gaudy architecture in St.

John's Archcathedral when I spied her. It was well over thirty years since she had bored the pants off me with talk about artesian wells and tectonic plates. But I couldn't risk detection so I developed a sudden urge to confess my sins. I stayed kneeling, rapt in prayer, until her party left the church. My legs took me a few hours to forgive me.

I'd missed a trick with 9/11. I could have disappeared almost effortlessly. I'd considered moving to the States but their immigration controls can be a little over zealous. I did not want to put my new identity to such a stringent test. So I remained in mainland Europe. I rented a dacha by a Russian lake. Apparently the owner only expected a summer let but I paid in advance for a whole year. It was a good country for my circumstances. No questions were asked as long as I paid in cash. And they loved dollars. The exchange rate was not too favourable but it was a small sacrifice to pay. It was time for me to consider the future. Could my luck hold or was a third death tempting fate or even gilding the lily? I was rather proud of my accomplishments and ability to cover my tracks. I didn't want to tarnish my unknown reputation. I idly scanned an old *Guinness Book of World Records* that I haggled over in a Moscow market. I was disappointed that there was not a highest number of recorded deaths for one individual section. I had nothing to aim for.

I discovered after a freezing winter alone that I possessed a strong need for achievement. I would almost call it a drive. So I took up ice fishing. I amused the locals by kitting out myself with all the necessary equipment. The local store was delighted to have such a big spender. Their words of advice were redundant since my linguistic ineptitude rendered their tips totally wasted. I found the Cyrillic script utterly impenetrable.

The coroner's report detailed how local residents had attempted to warn this plucky, yet foolhardy foreigner of the hazards of such a high-risk sport. It was common for participants in this extreme sport to go missing and to be found months or even years later deep in the permafrost. The insurance company coughed up quickly this time. I would certainly recommend them in the future. Unfortunately I wouldn't be able to use them again. They were rather fussy about that sort of thing. There was something in the small print about the same person not being able to claim twice for their death. Rather petty of them.

I decided it was time for a change of climate. I headed south and purchased a whole new wardrobe. I travelled light and after scouting possible nesting places I plumped for the Isle of Capri. It had a certain cachet in my mind and living there did not disappoint. After paying lip-service to the obvious tourist destinations, I soon crossed the Blue Grotto and a boat trip around the Gulf of Naples off my list. I settled in a charming little flat overlooking the Marina Piccola. It was true that I had grown weary of dressing every morning with at least five layers to avoid frostbite, yet even the many charms of this southern Italian paradise began to pall after a while. I grew restless.

The only way to stifle my overactive imagination and constant planning was to give myself over to my new passion. I became an addict of the cathode ray tube or whatever is the new-fangled, vital component of plasma televisions. I subscribed with my new identity to a dazzling amount of channels that my satellite dish beamed into my home. Naturally I learned quickly to sift through the viewing chaff on offer. I soon became quite an expert on Australian soap operas. If my anonymity were not quite so precious I could have been tempted to apply for *Mastermind.* 'The events and characters of *Neighbours* and *Home and Away*' would have been my specialist subject.

Despite the beautiful surroundings, my Italian haven provided me with no inspiration for a foolproof way of faking my own death for the fourth time. The somewhat limited appeal of *Ice Road Truckers* sparked off an idea that I found difficult to repress. My driving history was clean in many different names. I could easily study for my HGV licence. I rather fancied the idea of the long distance haulage journeys delivering essential supplies to grateful, isolated Alaskan communities. It would be on one such journey that my truck could lose control on a particularly icy stretch or my rig, as I learned they were called by their drivers, might attempt to fatefully cross a patch of thawing road in a desperate race against the onset of the summer melt. I had to stop watching that channel eventually as I knew that US border controls would be too officious.

So I turned my attention to a different part of the Americas. I started some research on the isthmus connecting the two American continents. Panama intrigued me. All I knew about it was its renown for hats. I soon became a fact junkie about its economy, exports, chaotic political history. I made plans to fly to South America. I figured that security wouldn't be so tight since half of Hitler's cronies seemed to have found it very easy to relocate there after the war. I would then travel up to my new home with some sightseeing thrown in. I had booked my ticket to Rio and was making an appointment for travel vaccinations when there was a curious item on the news. I suppose that I should have seen this as a sign at the time. I soon learned to despise the name of John Darwin. What a complete amateur he was. He made a pig's ear of faking his own death. I could have pointed out to him that he should never have allowed himself to be photographed. The canoe story was frankly preposterous. My plans were scuppered. Panama was now off the itinerary.

But I was never one for wasting anything and the ticket to Brazil was paid for, so I packed my bag once again. I checked into a modest hotel and awoke refreshed to sample the delights of this new city. I almost quibbled with the lady in the ticket office. I knew the cable car journey to the top of Sugarloaf Mountain took only three minutes and the cost of eleven dollars struck me as exorbitant. I now wish that I had followed my parsimonious instincts and declined the ascent. The following one hundred and eighty seconds sowed the seeds of my downfall.

There was no escaping her gaze. As I stepped into the glass capsule I lost interest in the sleek Italian design of my new means of transport. The anticipated delights of the effortless climb with its spectacular view no longer held my interest. My palms began sweating as I came face to face with my former geography teacher. Why was I cursed to bump into her again? Although of all my former teachers, her choice of subject made her the most likely to have developed a taste for wanderlust. She neither spoke nor attempted to grab my attention. Yet she conveyed that she knew. She just smiled and I knew the game was up, to use the American vernacular.

I couldn't wait for the return journey to come to a stop. Just before the doors opened, she reached out and handed me a piece of paper. It stated the name of her hotel with the word 'bar' and the time of 8 p.m. I could simply not turn up. I could book a flight to anywhere in the world rather than meet my potential nemesis. I knew that the message was an order and not a request. But I didn't have to do as she said. For heaven's sake, she'd lost what little power she had over me the day I left school.

I sat in my own hotel room and considered my options as calmly as possible. Flight was always a possibility but the constant readjustments were becoming a chore. I could turn up at the rendezvous and discover what she knew. Perhaps it was an elaborate flirtation and she didn't recognise the geographically-challenged teenager she had taunted in class. Maybe she was attracted to this man of mystery. If she turned out to be a blackmailer I could dispose of her. I'd done it to myself three times already. It might be fun to add another string to my bow.

*****

She had made a considerable effort with her appearance. Even after all these years it struck me as weird to see my former geography teacher sipping from a cocktail glass.

"Care to join me in a daiquiri?"

I nodded in agreement and she called out to the barman, "Two more please."

She seemed at ease swivelling on her bar stool. "You've done rather well for yourself. I would never have put you in the most likely to succeed category. I've been doing a little research since we bumped into each other again in the cable car. Fantastic views, weren't they?"

She wasn't expecting an answer and continued. "I took early retirement about ten years ago but I still receive the termly school magazine. It's mostly fundraising and statistics worthy of a cub reporter on *Pravda*. One day the new head will crow about his 110% exam pass rate. The little obituary written about you was rather touching. You did not seem to have achieved much, but I wasn't that surprised. I was, though, when I caught a glimpse of you in that church in Hungary–"

"Poland." I couldn't stop myself. Correcting a teacher was thrilling, especially on a point of geographical accuracy.

"Thank you. I wasn't entirely convinced it was you, but now I know. I was on one of those hideous coach trips where you are herded about from one tourist trap to another. I've since learned that travel should be savoured but unfortunately that is a costly pursuit. I long to visit the places that I have taught about and stay as long as I like. I won't burden you with my precarious pecuniary position but my pension is the wrong side of meagre. So you can imagine how surprised I was to see you today. It proved that my eyesight and memory are rather good. One does worry about these things as the years go by. I was wondering whether you could give me some advice."

I was taken aback. This wasn't where I thought the conversation would be heading. She took a handful of nuts from the bowl on the bar.

"What sort of advice are you seeking?"

She waited until she had finished chewing the peanuts in her mouth. "Financial."

"Well I'm afraid you've come to the wrong person. Perhaps your local bank has somebody who could advise you?"

"I think that you would be the very best person to help. You left school with very few formal qualifications and no apparent means to support yourself. Yet you seem to have carved out a comfortable existence. Perhaps you could provide me with some advice about life insurance for instance?"

The smile she gave me caused any doubt to evaporate. My lucrative scam was about to come to an end. I could run I suppose. Although she struck me as rather well-preserved, I still had twenty or possibly twenty-five years on her. I could outrun her. I could be at the airport within an hour.

She interrupted my thoughts. "I'm not a greedy woman. I don't intend to call the police. I would just like to share in your good fortune."

Now I understood – blackmail. I spoke the word out loud.

"Oh let's not talk like that."

"Well what would you call it?"

"I saw us entering into a business arrangement."

"What do I get out of it?"

"My silence and occasional company. Your existence, through necessity, must have become terribly lonely."

Oh dear, if she was expecting some sort of physical relationship then that was a step too far. I could cope with giving her money, I certainly had plenty to spare but the thought of –

She interrupted, "I simply meant that there must be times when you would like to share the secrets of your ingenuity. You've outwitted the authorities and yet have nobody to tell. To be brutally frank, my recollections of you in the classroom did not augur well for your future success. You were hardly my most promising pupil."

I suppose I should have been rather hurt. Everybody thinks that they are exceptional in some way or other. But she was right. I had passed through the corridors of my school unnoticed. No wall was emblazoned with the outward display of my academic prowess.

She continued, "I'm rather impressed with you. Beachy Head was a little obvious but do tell me how you managed to collect the insurance money yourself."

*****

That was a glorious evening – one of the best of my life. She only knew about one of my deaths. When I told her about the others she was the most agreeable audience and genuinely appeared impressed at my achievements. I was surprised at my own reaction. It was strange that even after all these years I should be so bothered about the approval of a former teacher. But the fact is that it meant a lot to me. She craved details and did not allow me to skate over any of my escapades. She was fascinated about the amount of research I had put into my plans. It was a relief to tell my story to another human being. Her proposal was simple. She would set up an account that we would call her travelling fund. I would make a monthly payment. The amount proposed was not excessive. If the money failed to turn up in her account she would inform the authorities of my crimes. She betrayed the sentimental side of her personality when she suggested an annual reunion. I agreed half-heartedly. I thought that sending each other postcards on a semi-regular basis would suffice. As a warning she told me that she had drafted a letter to her younger sister that afternoon. It contained a sealed envelope that should only be opened upon her death. This letter provided detailed information about my first faked death. This way, she pointed out with a big grin, I would have rather a vested interest in her continued good health.

After several more cocktails she responded favourably to my invitation to discover the city at night. Observers would have noticed a couple, perhaps mother and son, out for a night-time stroll – both in good spirits. I suggested we visit a hotel bar on Ipanema Beach to toast our collaboration. She liked the sound of that. We clinked our cocktail glasses and then stood enjoying the seaview from the seventh floor.

It was tragic how she fell from the beach bar balcony. That's what I told the police officer sent by the hotel to investigate her sudden death. I explained that, despite my warnings, she had insisted on leaning over the balcony to obtain a better view. The post-mortem revealed an excessive amount of alcohol in her blood. Therefore I escaped any suspicion. I'd never been much of a gambler. Poker had never appealed but there was something in her manner that told me she was bluffing about the letter to her sister. I took the risk.

I could have afforded to pay her a monthly stipend. But it was the principle of the matter. It struck me as rather immoral that she should profit from my hard work. But it was a great feeling to know that I'd left my mark on at least one teacher from my old school.

Being Colin

"When did you first meet Colin?"

"That's an easy one. April 26th. Heading towards our third anniversary. Leather or crystal, I looked it up. Rather a random combination."

"That's still seven months away."

"Yes, but I like to be prepared. Cub Scout code. Dib dib dib... Not really into all that though. The reality of sleeping under canvas with several other boys I found quite distasteful, and cooking our meals over open fires was positively Neanderthal."

"How old were you then?"

"Eight. Tried it for a couple of months. The green jumper was as itchy as hell. I remember poring over the handbook at the potential embroidery badges I could be awarded. Nothing I was interested in."

"What were your interests then?"

"Colouring. Writing stories and drawing the type of house I would live in with my future wife. I used to love to arrange my felt tips in colour order on my little desk. It drove me mad when my mother used one to scribble her shopping list. Such a careless woman. She would often leave the lids off. The set would be ruined."

"So you expected to marry a woman when you grew up?"

"Of course I did. What a daft question. I should have known you'd pick up on that."

She looks quite hurt now. I shouldn't be so mean. It's just that this slip of a girl is so predictable. She looks at me as if she feels my pain, has walked a mile in my shoes and all those other meaningless phrases implying supposed empathy. How old is she? Twenty-three, twenty-four? Is this the best they can get? I know everybody has to start somewhere but couldn't they have given me somebody a little more senior?

"I'm sorry, Liz. Please forgive me. We were brought up on a diet of happy ever after films with huge weddings. As a boy, I was Rock Hudson in search of his Miss Day. And all along I was a Doris."

Good grief. I should never have been so conciliatory. Now she's behaving like a demented nodding dog. She thinks she's cracked me. The poor love is spouting some psychobabble about role models, positive images and homophobia. She'll be quoting page numbers from *A Beginner's Guide to Sociology* next. If I start counting the tiles on the wall behind her maybe I'll be able to ride this one out. Relief, I only got to 167 and she's stopped.

"Well that brings us to the end of our therapeutic hour."

Liz smiles. I had remarked in the first session that the appointment had been curtailed abruptly. She had patiently explained that each session was allotted fifty minutes so as to allow her to reflect on her client's predicament and to prepare for the next one. Why call it an hour then? I feel cheated.

"I will see you tomorrow, Stephen. Same time."

I smile this time and leave the room. I'm desperate to see what she's written about me. I wonder if I fascinate her. I hope so. Perhaps Liz will be able to make me the focus of her first book. I have always dreamed of being a *cause celebre*. I would much prefer it if she wrote her comments into a hard backed jotter instead of the cheap A4 pad with pre-punched holes to add me to her file. It would make me feel more permanent and important.

I choose to walk around the garden before lunch. I manage to steer clear of the other residents and make my way towards the vegetable patch. I focus on the courgettes. Liz would, no doubt, draw an easy conclusion from that one. I would never have made the connection with a phallus. I was merely interested in how quickly they are growing. I've only been here a week and some of these are in danger of being taken to court under the Trade Descriptions Act. Have they become marrows yet?

We have to take turns here. I had been assigned the breakfast shift. I felt I had excelled at the place settings. I am sure that the reason that nobody congratulated me on the water lily was the early hour. Maybe at lunch or supper, which they insist on calling tea here, my origami skills would have garnered greater appreciation. Nobody seems to be a morning person here. Even by lunchtime, many of my fellow guests do not seem to have shifted up the necessary gear to participate fully in the day.

I would have elected a table on my own to eat. I am not a social being, especially when food is concerned. Mass catering does tend towards the bland. That I can cope with. It is the table manners of the others I find difficult to bear, many of whom are not terribly well acquainted with cutlery. Unfortunately, all the dining chairs are arranged around rectangular tables in a refectory style. Liz says it is to encourage us to interact with each other. What a hideous turn of phrase. Why can't she say, talk, chat, converse? No, it has to be 'interact'. I have learned that if I am one of the first in the lunch queue, I can wolf down by meal before my table has begun to fill up. The danger of burning my tongue is miniscule, as the average temperature of so-called 'hot' meals is at best tepid, bordering on cold.

My macaroni cheese has developed a skin by the time I am ready to eat it. I have to say a short prayer of thanks before every meal. I have a strict hierarchy of things for which to be grateful, the last and most important being Colin. As I open my eyes and pick up my fork, check its level of cleanliness before attempting to put it anywhere near my food, my luck fails me.

"If I'm not interrupting, may I join you? I couldn't help noticing that you were praying."

This is all I need, but the only offensive thing about this woman is her taste in cardigans. I turn my attention to eating but she clearly wants to 'interact'.

"Have you been here long?"

"I arrived last week."

"Is your room comfortable?"

"Well, a Jacuzzi and a few silk throws wouldn't go amiss. I wouldn't object if they provided me with a decently sprung mattress. But the rates are very reasonable so I mustn't complain."

That almost made her choke on her beetroot salad. When her laughter subsided she continued.

"You have a sense of humour."

"Guilty as charged. It's one of the qualities Colin most admires."

"Who's he?"

I take an overly long time to swallow my mouthful. I enjoy the dramatic pause. My luncheon companion strikes me as possibly a little prudish.

"He's my partner."

Not a flicker.

"You must miss him terribly."

"I do. Apparently, they frown on visitors from outside, but I'm sure Colin will find a way. He's frightfully persuasive when he puts his mind to something. How about you? Been here long?"

"About four years."

Now it's my turn to almost choke on the overcooked pasta. The chef is clearly not on speaking terms with Al Dente. I rapidly reappraise her. She looks extremely well adjusted to me. I had been assured that stays of over six months were relatively rare. She must have bucketfuls of what Liz would call 'unresolved issues'.

"Four years is rather a long time. Don't tell me the food's better than at home."

"I cook for myself or occasionally I guilt trip my partner into making a meal."

"Are you here on day release then?"

This causes another outburst of suppressed hilarity.

"Oh no. I work here"

She pulls her offending cardigan to one side to reveal a staff badge pinned at a rakish angle on her blouse. This is all I need. She's the chaplain.

"That's why you were drawn to me praying."

"Am I the answer to your prayer?"

For one truly ghastly moment I believe she thinks she has been divinely sent. The smile betrays her.

"I'm pulling your leg. I'm Sally, by the way."

Sally has suddenly become one of them. I no longer feel her equal. I hope that I do not communicate this. She coaxes rather more information out of me than I usually share with a stranger.

"So, Stephen, how long do you think you'll be here?"

"I'm not really sure. I suppose until they find out what's been wrong with me. I was dreading it was going to be all raffia and basket weaving."

"We tend to save that for the extremely desperate cases."

I'm liking this woman a little more.

Sally peels an orange and offers me some of the segments. I surprise myself by accepting. I normally don't do sharing. The tanginess of the fruit catches me by surprise. Seedless, thank goodness. I would have felt awkward spitting out orange pips in front of her, no matter how discretely I had managed it.

"I have my first group therapy session this afternoon. I'm not sure what to expect. I worry that I'll either clam up or go the other way and perform. I just love a captive audience. I think that my strategy will be to listen to my peers to begin with."

"Wise move."

"So, what are your duties here?"

"It's a training post."

"But four years is an awfully long time."

"The truth is that I feel that God still wants me here. You'd understand that."

I must have a puzzled expression.

"I assumed that you are a spiritual person; saying grace before your meal."

"Oh that, it's just become a habit over the years."

I was beginning to lose concentration and was thinking of my disappointment that I had still not encountered an experienced professional during my stay. This included the catering staff.

"Would you describe yourself as someone of faith?"

"I don't tend to give it much thought. I'm far too busy with more pressing issues, like who's going to win the *X Factor* or which tie to wear."

"I shall back down gracefully. I hope your session goes well this afternoon. If you ever feel the need to talk, my hours are pinned up outside the chapel. We also have a non-denominational service each Sunday. Thank you for allowing me to eat with you. I'm off to catch up on my e-mails."

"The scourge of the 21st century."

I think that's what you're meant to say. I am not terribly au fait with computer stuff. As she stands up, Sally reaches out her hand. I shake it.

It is the first time I have touched another human being since I arrived.

*****

I hate arriving late for anything. Missing the first two minutes of a feature film ruins it for me. So I am outside the group counselling suite a full quarter of an hour before the session is due to start. I walk along the corridors with a pretend sense of purpose and return to the suite every couple of minutes. When I come back after the fourth mini stroll there is a bearded man arranging the mismatched chairs into a vaguely circular formation. I have seen him before with a clipboard in the refectory so he's probably the facilitator. I have learned this word from the information pack in my room. I allow myself one more circuit of the corridors. When I return, almost everybody is settled. This at least means that I shall not be committing the cardinal sin of sitting in somebody else's chair. Considering their sloth and distinct lack of pep, I'm impressed by the time-keeping of my fellow inmates.

I don't know how I managed to control myself. The beard with the clipboard was straight out of central casting. Five minutes into the session I realised that I was in the presence of seriously deranged individuals. It was similar to encountering a drunk at a party. You may have had a few drinks yourself but faced with a person with slurred speech and an inability to co-ordinate their own body you soon sober up. I leave the room at the end of the session with the profound feeling that there isn't much wrong with me. Sure, I have done some things that strike others as strange, but I'm not the one with suicidal tendencies or multiple personalities. I also possess a healthy respect for matches. After that experience, I feel I am sitting in Accident and Emergency with a broken fingernail. I shall save this for Liz tomorrow.

I go to my room and catch up with my correspondence. Top of my list is Colin, of course. I scribble quite an accurate and humorous account of the afternoon. This will tickle him. Then a few short notes. I ought to write to my few friends who bothered to turn up for that pathetic excuse for a trial. I've been deliciously vague with my neighbours. I mentioned I was going travelling and not to expect me back too soon. I started to believe it partially myself. I had made sure that I returned home after frequent shopping visits with armfuls of glossy holiday brochures.

I'm having no problems sleeping here. I haven't got a decent photograph of the both of us, so I've spliced two separate ones together. I don't think you can see the join. The trouble is that my head seems so much bigger than Colin's. I've put it in a silver frame of my mother's. It's the first thing I see in the morning and the last thing before I turn out the light. I don't kiss it or anything. That would be daft.

I wake up within a fifteen-minute range every morning, regardless of when I went to sleep. I have a fairly free day today. I have my five sixths of an hour with Liz to look forward to and little else. I don't feel any anxiety around my sessions with Liz. I'm probably doing her more good if the truth be told although she doesn't open up to me terribly often. I'll have to see about that.

As usual, I am early and waiting outside her cubbyhole of an office. Ten minutes to go. I should have brought a book. It's weird though, but I'm finding it difficult to concentrate on novels at the moment, which is a new development. Maybe I'll mention that to her. She pokes her head out two and a half minutes after our appointment should have begun. Is she playing mind games with me? Unless her previous client was a contortionist and had managed to exit through her single office window she has deliberately kept me waiting; her paperwork taking precedence over her allocated time with me. I choose not to bring this up since this would be playing straight into her hands.

After the pleasantries have been exchanged, she dives right in.

"I'm keen to explore your creativity today, Stephen. You talked about writing yesterday."

"Well, I've begun to write poetry. I never thought I was the type. I'm self-taught."

This clearly delights her.

"Have you ever shared your work with anybody? Colin for instance?"

"No, it's still for my own consumption. I haven't the confidence to show anyone else. It would be so difficult to allow Colin to read it."

"Why's that? Surely he wants to read what you've written."

"It's just not his sort of thing. Of course, he would pretend he liked it. Colin's very polite, but he would much prefer to be reading a DIY magazine or one about cars."

"Have you ever thought of joining a group or possibly approaching a publisher?"

"No, it's strictly for my own pleasure. I don't think it's terribly commercial. You see, it doesn't all rhyme. It's not the kind of thing you would see on a Hallmark card. When I write it out in best I like to illuminate the first letter of each stanza. That's poetry talk for a verse."

"Like a monk from the Middle Ages."

"Yes, I suppose so."

I can tell she's exhausted that topic. I wonder what's next.

"You attended your first group therapy session yesterday. How was it?"

"I expect you want honesty, so here goes: What a bunch of self-absorbed freaks. I mean, some of them are so slow. You can practically hear the cogs in their brains go round as they figure out what to say next."

"Many of our clients are on medication to equalise their moods. Your stay here will be much easier if you appreciate that we cater for a wide range of needs."

"You mean I should not be so critical of the other inmates."

"We prefer the term client, Stephen."

"Well, I believe in calling a spade a spade, Liz. Some of the people here are barking mad. I'm surprised you feel safe in a confined space with some of those nutters, even if they are wearing chemical overcoats."

"I'm not finding this terribly productive, Stephen. Let's talk about Colin. Are you angry with him?"

"Why on earth should I be?"

"According to my notes, it was Colin who reported you to the police."

"No, you've got it all wrong, Liz. That's just the way the papers twisted things."

"But he testified against you in court. I have the transcripts here. He claimed that you were harassing him."

"He loves me."

"So why did he take out a court injunction against you, banning you from going within 250 metres of his home and place of work?"

"That was his so-called girlfriend. The bitch was jealous of what we had. She wanted to get between us."

"But at no point during the trial did Colin say anything other than he loved his girlfriend and found your behaviour menacing and intimidating."

"He's weak. He says things for an easy life. I've tried to talk to him about that."

"You were accused of stealing things from Colin."

Liz looks down at her notes.

"Articles of clothing..."

"That's a lie. He used to lend me things, leave them around where he knew I would find them."

"You took his mobile phone."

"We'd had one of our arguments. I wanted to teach him a lesson."

"Colin claimed that the only contact together was when he serviced your car almost two and a half years ago."

"See, friends do things for each other."

"But he was a mechanic at the garage. You paid the company he worked for."

"I don't know what you're implying."

Liz leans towards me. I notice that one of her bra straps is quite grubby.

"If you want to get better Stephen, you will have to start by being honest. If you want us to help you–"

"You're just like all the others. Nobody believes me."

"The judge was lenient by allowing you to come here, considering the evidence. Colin's girlfriend was traumatised by the letters you wrote as well as the phone messages."

"They were just for fun. She didn't have a sense of humour."

"You threatened to kill her on several occasions. The police had Colin's phone tapped. If you refuse to co-operate, it will be a custodial sentence for you."

I couldn't stay in that room any longer and listen to all those lies again. Fortunately, I made my way outside without anybody seeing me cry. Everyone is ganging up on me just like before. Somebody behind me coughs. It's Sally.

"I didn't know whether you wanted to be left alone. I'll go if you like."

"No, it's OK."

"Nothing serious I hope. Is it about Colin?"

I'm glad she remembers his name.

"Yes. There's been a misunderstanding. He can't come and see me for a while."

"Work commitments?"

"Yes, something like that."

Making a Hash of Things

"Darling, what a clever idea. We'll see you tomorrow. Must dash or my lasagne will be beyond crisp and you know what your father's like about his food. See you tomorrow. Kisses to the boys." I replace the phone and take a deep breath. Now I have to break it to him.

As I begin to serve up our supper he strides into the kitchen in search of a corkscrew. I begin the charm offensive. "How about a bottle of fizz tonight?"

This stops him in his tracks. Forty-seven years together makes us likely candidates for *Mastermind*, with each other as our specialist subject. He knows I'm up to something, even while my back is turned and I'm wrestling with the oven door.

"Broken something? Or have I forgotten a significant date we're meant to be celebrating?" he asks sarcastically.

"Stop being so suspicious. I just thought that since it's the start to the weekend and we have Jed's birthday party tomorrow, we could—"

"Don't remind me. I still haven't abandoned all hope of coming up with a plausible excuse to get out of it."

"Don't be like that, darling. Susie's expecting us. I've just got off the phone with her. Besides, we couldn't wish for a better son-in-law. He's so good with the children."

I wish I could take that last bit back. He'll take it as a criticism of his parenting. I've explained it countless times. Things were different when we were younger; fathers were expected to provide, and be the ultimate deterrent. Anyway, he detests all that touchy-feely stuff. I know perfectly well why he isn't looking forward to the party. Jed's parents will naturally be there and let's just say that since the wedding both sides of the family have not seen eye to eye. As long as we keep away from discussing religion, politics, or pretty much any topic of conversation apart from the weather, we tend to be alright.

He doesn't need much encouragement to open up a bottle of champagne. We sit across each other at the table. I dish out the food and he pours the drinks. Over the years, we have reached an agreement about the division of labour; although it's not entirely equal. As he raises his glass to me, he smiles. "I was thinking we can pop in there about three, do the rounds and be out of there within the hour, ninety minutes tops. What have you bought him? Anything half decent?"

"I thought you were getting him something?" I can't quite carry this one off convincingly. He sticks his tongue out at me. Purchasing presents is decidedly on my list of household chores. It's no use; I'm going to have to tell him. I try not to wince as I say, "There's been a slight change of plan."

This causes him to lay down his cutlery. "What?" he manages to ask, once he stops chewing.

"Well, you know you're always complaining about their 'at homes'?"

"Ghastly, yes, where we all sit around like spare parts–"

I cut him off from one of his familiar set pieces and say, "Susie fancied trying something new. She wants to have a surprise barbeque."

"But they live in a second floor flat."

My husband can be dense sometimes. I can see him trying to work this one out. After a few seconds he splutters, "Good God, they don't want us to have it here, do they? All the great unwashed traipsing over my flower beds. I couldn't–"

"Stop worrying about your precious fuchsias. They're not coming here."

"So where are they having it?"

Here goes. I swallow hard and then announce with as much enthusiasm as I can muster, "On the beach."

"But it'll be packed and–"

I interrupt and explain to him that it is going to be in the evening and yes, it will be late for the children and yes, I know he doesn't like going out at night. But it's our daughter's decision and we will grin and bear it.

"I shall pray for rain."

"You can be a miserable old sod at times. Besides, it might be fun."

"That really would be the surprise part."

I prepare for a protracted sulk from him.

As I load the dishwasher I wonder what I can do to cheer him up. He never used to be like this. When we were courting he would surprise me constantly. I no longer recognise the man who sent me get well telegrams when I had raging toothache, or the impromptu picnics. Now suggesting trying a different supermarket is a possible hanging offence.

He barely acknowledges me throughout our predictable evening routine. We half watch the old gogglebox, while he wrestles with a crossword and I catch up on some mending. To our friends, he always insists he watches hardly any television. Unfortunately it's been our constant companion over the years, releasing us from the need to communicate. Tonight is no exception. It's normally a race as to who falls asleep first in their respective armchairs. He wins this evening.

I can't remember the year we decided upon separate bedrooms. He has to get up a lot in the night and besides, he hates all my cushions and throws I like to have on the bed. I can hear him snore even through the wall with the door closed. It's sort of comforting and intensely irritating at the same time.

*****

"Good morning."

He grunts a reply as he twiddles with the dial on the radio at the kitchen table. I know his game. He's surfing radio channels for a pessimistic weather forecast. He's out of luck. I've checked the newspaper and the breakfast television news and they all promise a weekend of unusually high temperatures with no threat of rain or even the lightest of winds. I place a plate of buttered toast next to the radio and barely get a response. I take his brief glance at the plate as a thank you.

Eavesdropping on a phone call to our daughter later that morning infuriates him further. I offer to pay for the cost of the drinks for the party. This causes him to exclaim, "Are we made of money?"

Fortunately I cover the receiver so she could not have heard. She is insistent that they can manage. I worry as neither of them is working full-time, but she tells me everything is under control and that we should simply come along and enjoy ourselves. I expect her to add 'for once' but mercifully she doesn't. Perhaps our daughter is blissfully unaware of how much her father hates these events.

I take a trip to the supermarket alone to buy some food. The least I can do is provide some fresh salads for the barbeque. I feel better turning up with a contribution, rather than just a present.

I chop the vegetables as he noisily strains over a Sudoku puzzle at the kitchen table. We have now officially not spoken to each other for almost twenty hours. I can't recall whether this is a record when he breaks the silence.

"Can't you tell her I'm sick?"

"If you want to lie to our daughter, that's fine. Go ahead and do it. Just don't involve me."

"What on earth are we going to wear? God only knows what we'll end up treading in? Owners never pick up after their dogs. It's a disgrace. We'll probably be crapped on by seagulls."

I don't bother to answer him on specifics. "We're going and that's final and if it's the only thing you do, you will present to each and everyone there a happy and smiling face."

He knows me well enough. I'm not bluffing. He goes upstairs and takes his frustration out on the bedroom furniture. The drawers and doors have become accustomed to his rough treatment over the years.

*****

We live near enough to the beach to walk. At least that means we can both have a drink. He grumbles about the quantity of Tupperware we are having to take, although I make sure that I have the heavier bags.

"I bet we don't get these back, or we'll be given the wrong lids."

I point out to him that each container and lid is separately labelled. I've never known him take so much interest in kitchen equipment. I usually have to speed up to keep up with his brisk walking pace but this evening he's positively dawdling.

As we turn the last corner, the sea wind carries the sound of music from the beach. He mutters something about noise pollution, but I choose to ignore him. There's a small crowd there already. When we are about a hundred yards away our grandsons recognise us and race towards us. Their innocent play and requests for magic tricks will occupy my grouch of a husband while I help to lay out the food. I compliment Susie on the arrangements. She has attached balloons to the trestle tables and her sons have made a spectacular *Happy Birthday* banner with multicoloured hand prints. They must have had fun making that.

"What wonderful food. Where is the birthday boy then?" I ask.

She explains that his friends have taken him to the pub and they're not due to join us for at least another half hour. The timing will be perfect, she adds, since it will just be getting dark and the fairy lights will be even more effective. She wants it to be perfect for him. She hugs me. I am touched by how much they always seem to want to please each other. I can't imagine my husband organising a surprise party for me nowadays. Mind you, I think I'd die of embarrassment if he ever did. The notion is ridiculous.

I stand alongside Susie. There is precious little to do. I look down at the shore line and see my husband in teacher mode. He's trying to show our grandsons how to skim stones. He only makes two ripples at a time. I worry he's lost the knack. He gets so crotchety so easily these days. I don't want him spoiling things.

A succession of people arrive. They are laden with presents, cards, food and bottles. Soon there are over a hundred of us, all ages. I didn't know they knew so many people. I am introduced but I give up on remembering names. Quite a few people are smoking. Susie normally worries (my husband says overreacts) about her children inhaling smoke. She doesn't seem too bothered about it this evening. Strange, it doesn't smell like regular cigarettes; must be herbal ones. Goodness me, she just took a puff herself.

My husband comes up to me. He seems very relaxed. He offers me a small biscuit from his plate and says, "Try one of these, they're delicious. I've had half a dozen already. You must ask Susie for the recipe."

My daughter was never keen on cooking as a child. Maybe it's motherhood that's brought on this new interest.

My husband looks around him with a look of approval, which for once is not grudging. "Pretty impressive set-up they have here. Lights and music rigged up to that generator and a backup one too."

His admiration is interrupted by spontaneous shouts and cheers which drown out the music. Our son-in-law appears, flanked by his parents and friends. He must have known that Susie was plotting something, but he acts the part well of the duped husband. He's hoisted into the air by three of them. Somebody places a paper crown on his head and the children lead us all in singing "Happy Birthday". I'm amazed at my husband joining in so heartily. He's even one of the crowd calling for a speech. Reluctantly, Jed agrees. I'm impressed by his easy eloquence and the warm reception of the gathered guests. There is rapturous applause when he finishes. This turns into whoops of delight as he kisses our daughter for what seems an immodest length of time. I usually find this level of public intimacy distasteful, but I'm really envious of their ability to be so comfortable together. The children don't seem to notice. They're too busy having fun.

I crouch down and pick up some cans and plastic cups which have fallen on to the ground. I might as well make myself useful. As I look for a bin bag (I know I should have brought some) Jed takes my hand and all of a sudden we're dancing. The music is unfamiliar to me but it just sounds right in this uncustomary hot weather. I'm not sure of the right steps; I just sway. Of course, I am frightfully self-conscious but as I look around, nobody seems to judge or even notice me; they are all just having a good time. The children are jigging about, running in and out and between groups of grown-ups. A couple of our grandsons' friends have made a camp under one of the trestle tables. Funny, normally I would panic about it collapsing on top of them and a frantic rush to A&E. But in the fading light, with shadows from the flickering candles, it simply looks like fun.

I catch a glimpse of my husband. He's dancing with Jed's mother. Oh dear, I do hope he's behaving himself. What's this? Jed's father good naturedly tries to cut in and the three of them all share a joke. I'm too far away to hear exactly what has been said but they all seem to be laughing for an extraordinary length of time. The doctor has warned my husband about his alcohol intake. I begin to worry. I excuse myself from Jed and work my way over to my husband. When I reach him, I whisper in his good ear, "I think you've had enough, dear."

He assures me he's only had two glasses. Obviously I believe him, but I haven't seen him this...happy, in years.

Susie introduces me to some of her friends. They seem ever so interested in my opinions. I haven't talked so much for ages. I meet a lovely couple of women. I think they're sisters at first. They have the same hairstyles. I am surprised to hear that one of them is a police officer. The artist is my favourite. He is ever so animated about his latest project. It's lovely to hear somebody talk with so much passion about his work. He makes things out of objects people throw away. I like the idea of that. He is quite brazen about it. He tells me how he goes scavenging through skips. He smiles when I tell him to be careful. He has lovely teeth. It makes you see the point of recycling. He's even invited me to visit his studio some time. As he hands me his card, Jed passes by and whispers in my ear, "Your secret's safe with me. I shan't tell your husband." When I realise what he means I turn but he's gone. I blush. Surely he doesn't think that I'd be unfaithful? Besides, this artist is at least twenty years younger.

One of Susie's neighbours tells me about her job. I don't quite understand what she does. It's something to do with computers and web design. She asks me what I do for a living. I laugh. She doesn't seem to understand that I don't need to work. My husband's pension is very generous. She wonders whether I get bored but I reel off the list of things I do. I've got plenty to keep me busy. There are the flowers at the church, the ladies I shop for, the garden of course, and looking after a four bedroom house is a job in itself. She seems a bit embarrassed and changes the subject. She remarks how lucky I am to have a son-in-law like Jed, and how good he is with the children. I agree.

At first, I think my watch is playing up. Then I realise it's correct and we've been at the party for over three hours. The whole evening is like something out of a film. Everybody seems to get on well. The storm lanterns create a beautiful glow and illuminate patches of the beach. The music has been turned down and many people are sitting around in groups, but there's no sign of people planning to leave. There's a lot of laughter. Someone has lit a fire. I hope they don't get into trouble. I'm sure the council wouldn't approve. I consider mentioning it to Susie but decide against it. I don't want to put a dampener on things. One chap with long hair is strumming his guitar. I don't recognise the tunes but it sounds pretty.

I stand in front of the tables and as I match lids to containers, I'm grabbed from behind. It's my husband. I listen carefully to check whether his speech is slurred as he announces, "We're off sailing next weekend!"

"But you've never been in a boat in your life, unless you count the Isle of Wight ferry when the children were young."

He goes on to explain how we are meeting up with Jed's parents next Saturday morning, adding, "Just because we're knocking on doesn't mean we can't be open to new experiences. I was thinking; if we get the taste for it we could get a boat of our own."

Is this really my husband speaking? I link arms with him and kiss his cheek. He kisses me back on the lips. I am simply stunned. We are in uncharted territory.

"Let's get you home, Captain."

I wonder what he'll be like tomorrow.

Professional Smile

"What are you doing that for? Your shooting practice night isn't until Wednesday."

Fortunately his wife stopped him as he attempted to load his air-pistol. He hesitated before he spoke. "I was just…er…cleaning it, Sandra."

"You were doing no such thing, Roger."

She gave him one of her looks.

"I was just going to send out a warning shot. I was hoping to scare him a bit. It's probably the only day of this wash-out of a summer and it's ruined by some so-called musician murdering a perfectly good tune."

"Murder is an unfortunate choice of word. You could've killed him."

"I just wanted to give him a little fright. It wouldn't have hurt…that much. Modern jazz, I ask you? Ruining my Sunday afternoon with his bloody saxophone. I'm not even sure his balcony was within range."

This didn't seem to impress her. He put the pistol away into his case.

She stood in the doorway and decided to attempt to be conciliatory. "Can I help you get ready? That bow-tie is ever so fiddly."

"I can manage perfectly well on my own, thank you very much. Besides, we've got ages."

"Not really. We have to leave in half an hour."

Sandra knew that retreat was her best option at this point. They dressed in separate rooms in silence. After years of experience, she knew it was her role to break the ice. "You look very smart, darling."

He grunted and muttered something about her dress being nice. Sandra decided not to press the issue.

"When's the car getting here, Roger?"

He looked at his wristwatch. "It's due in ten minutes. Just time for a stiff drink. After all, it is Mahler tonight. Joining me?"

"Yes please."

He poured two generous gin and tonics and they clinked glasses.

"Why on Earth couldn't they invite us to something like *South Pacific* – a show with tunes? You could come out of that humming any one of the songs. It would even put a smile on the face of a miserable old sod like me."

"Now, that would be a miracle." She blew him an air kiss. "Only teasing, Roger."

The driver was parked outside. He knew better than to sound his horn. Roger locked up the house as Sandra confirmed the venue with the chauffeur.

In the back of the car they sat in companionable silence and gazed out of the darkened windows. After a few minutes, he spoke – "Why don't we make our excuses and duck out of this one? There's a *Morse* marathon on the box tonight. We could both put our feet up and 'chillax' in the immortal words of our dear Prime Minister. We could have a take-away. You wouldn't even have to cook."

"Thank you kindly, Sir. After the Sunday lunch I slaved over today for ten of us, the kitchen is most definitely closed. Anyway, they always have food at these things if we get to the reception on time. You know that you have to show your face."

"You know what it's like though; all that poncy finger food and that mindless small talk."

"And you will do it all with a smile on your face."

They arrived at the concert hall and as soon as Roger left the car, his professional smile became fixed on his face and remained there until the driver came back for them at the end of the evening. As they drove off he began his rant.

"Call that food? I wouldn't give it to a dog. Thinking about it, it probably was dog. And who was that dreadful woman? I couldn't give her the slip. She wouldn't stop talking and then she turns out to be sitting next to me all evening. Surely, we could have swopped seats?"

"Now that would have been rude Roger. You know perfectly well that she was the wife of the conductor."

"I can't believe we had to sit through that depressing tripe. The second half seemed to last for hours."

"Well, just be grateful that it wasn't Wagner's *Ring Cycle*."

"It's just not fair. I never get to do what I want to do. Nothing ever seems to go right. I've had enough. It's been a miserable excuse of a summer. First there was the crass wall to wall coverage of the Jubilee. The Beeb wouldn't know what gravitas meant if it woke up in bed with it. Euro 2012 was a travesty. For God's sake, who'd have thought we'd invented the game. Then Team GB's disastrous effort at that embarrassment of an Olympic Games. Beaten in the medal table by Luxembourg. Let's gloss over the ignominy of Murray's Wimbledon attempt. It's been a lousy summer – test matches have been rained off and the first and only decent day of good weather was wrecked by a jazz saxophonist. I expect we've got something awful like the ballet booked for tomorrow night.'

"No, actually, that's on Tuesday. According to your schedule you have the Rumanian mime troupe tomorrow evening."

"Oh God, that's all I need. That bloody Marcel Marceau has a lot to answer for. I swear if any of them come on with clown's make-up and start pretending they're trapped in a box I shall get up and leave."

"You know you'll do no such thing. You'll sit through it all and congratulate them at the end. Now, calm down, darling. I know exactly what you need."

She opened her handbag and handed him a brown paper bag. He breathed in and out several times and after a few minutes his face no longer quite resembled the colour of a beetroot.

"That's better. The doctor's warned you not to get yourself worked up."

Roger sat, looking sheepish, in the back of the car. "I'm sorry. I feel pretty foolish now. Thanks for stopping me. I just get so worked up. Everything's on top of me at the moment. You're ever so good for me, old girl," as he placed his hand on hers.

"Less of the old, thank you very much. Besides I know you so well. It's like this every year. You'll be happy when you're back at work, darling. When does term begin again?"

"You know perfectly well that it's not called that. You don't know what it's like to be Sports and Culture Secretary; this year of all years. The timing's awful. It's probably the worst moment in history to have this job. Everything's gone wrong for us. I'd rather have been in charge of prisons or sewage facilities. It wasn't my fault that some imbecile in the department signed off a billion pound scheme to promote Shakespeare in Swahili around our nation's primary schools. The press had a field day with that one, especially during our time of austerity. I can't be expected to check every decimal point. If the boss hadn't ordered a three line whip to ensure all government ministers 'staycationed'–ghastly phrase–we would be in the South of France like a shot. Apparently we're all in this together. Parliament doesn't open until the end of next month.'

"Well I shall be counting the days."

Tammy Rules

Her few remaining friends had offered to help. But Cathy had declined. She couldn't bear the thought of being pitied. Besides, she might need to call in favours in the future. That would be a test of friendship, when the case came to court. The lawyer had repeated that she must remain optimistic. Should it come to court, he would always remind her.

She wouldn't be deterred from the school run. Cathy was toughening up. The anonymous calls, emails and texts were easy to handle. She simply changed all email addresses and bought new SIM cards. Handwritten angry notes stuffed under her windscreen wipers were plentiful. She no longer bothered to read the words. She just didn't want her children to see them. Her mother's answer was easy – move. Cathy should uproot her family and flee. This was all her family said about the situation. If that didn't scream guilt then Cathy wasn't sure what did.

Cathy had learned to time it perfectly every afternoon. She parked a street away from the school. Her son would collect his two younger sisters and cross the road with the lollypop lady. As soon as they were safely strapped in, she drove off, avoiding any contact with other parents. It had been difficult to explain to her six and eight year old daughters why they no longer received party invitations.

The children knew better than to race upstairs to see their father. They had discovered recently that he didn't like to be disturbed. His office had become his bedsit after the allegations. Cathy had told them that Daddy needed to work late into the night, which meant he needed to sleep in a separate room to Mummy.

She had a well-established routine. While the children had a snack at the kitchen table, she would go through their book bags, ostensibly to recover any communication from the school. She had had to become doubly efficient to ensure her maternal credentials were not called into question. A missed consent form or parent teacher appointment would not assist her husband in the dock. There was always a good chance that a particularly vicious parent or even staff member might plant a hate-filled message in one of her children's bags.

Her son had lingered in the kitchen while his sisters had raced into the living room to watch television.

"What did Dad do?"

She couldn't meet his gaze. Why was she feeling so guilty?

"It's all been a huge misunderstanding, darling."

Cathy hoped that this would be sufficient. Unfortunately, her son stood his ground and carried on.

"They're all saying that Dad looked at some dirty pictures on his computer. Is that why that lady came to speak to me at school? She went on about touching. Good ones and bad ones."

"Some nasty person put some horrible stuff on our computer. Probably somebody who's jealous of your father at work. You know how clever he is. Now, let me tidy up in here. Go and join your sisters."

He didn't budge. Not until the first tear appeared. Then he blurted out,

"Is he going to go to prison?"

"Of course not."

Cathy moved in to hug her son but he turned and ran up the stairs. He probably did not want his mother to see him crying.

As she unloaded the dishwasher Cathy felt the urge to cry herself but bit her bottom lip. The metallic taste in her mouth was bitter. She needed to talk to somebody. But who could she trust? Were therapists duty bound to report crimes? She turned on the radio as a means of distraction. She recognised the twang of Tammy Wynette. Cathy had always hated country music and its cheap sentimentality. But she stood in her kitchen holding a fistful of cutlery while Tammy sang her heart out. She listened while the singer told Cathy to stand by her man, pointing out along the way that sometimes it was hard to be a woman.

The children came rushing downstairs at the sound of the radio being thrown against the unforgiving tiled floor.

"Silly Mummy dropped the radio on the floor. Be careful, there might be little pieces on the floor. I'll just get the hoover out. I'll call you when supper's ready."

The girls skipped back upstairs but her son was not convinced. He wanted to stay and help but Cathy insisted he left her to it.

"It's my mess. I have to clear it up."

As he reluctantly followed his sisters upstairs, Cathy wondered if she was just speaking about the smashed radio.

*****

After she'd fed her children, she made a meal tray for her husband. She left it on the floor outside his room. They had made an unspoken agreement to communicate as seldom as possible. She often heard him in the kitchen at night once she'd gone to bed. Her husband had been driven nocturnal. The legal advice had been that he should remain in the marital home at all costs or the prosecution would pounce on his departure to strengthen their case.

Cathy had learned to switch part of herself off. She simply needed to be strong for her children and survive the next few months. She operated on a functional basis. Cathy became an autopilot mum. She wasn't doing it for him. During one of their rare conversations her husband had told her he sensed she was coming around to forgiving him. She calmly told him not to flatter himself. That was never going to happen.

Weeks ago she'd been unloading the car after a supermarket run. When she reached for the last two carrier bags she saw an unfamiliar child's shoe. Cathy would never buy that kind of fashionable footwear. After a sleepless night, she'd disposed of it the next day at the council tip. When she'd told her husband, he'd just said 'Thanks'. He'd tried to smile but he turned away. He couldn't face her.

Then she knew.

Pieces of Pyrex

Roy waited before making the call. He had never had dealings with the police before. But it was now a quarter to ten in the evening and Sally had not returned home. It was a school night after all.

"For Christ's sake, call them," said his wife. Maureen had already rung around all of her daughter's closest friends. Now she sat in the lounge.

Nobody had seen Sally.

"You're too frightened to bother anyone, aren't you? Your own daughter could be…"

That was enough. Roy went into the kitchen and dialled. Maureen hated his telephone voice.

"She's fourteen…no not during the week…never done this before." Roy hung up. "They're sending someone over now."

Roy took up his position in the bay window as Maureen lit up another Embassy in the kitchen.

The constable arrived within twenty minutes. After introductions and formalities, Roy accompanied her on a search of the house.

"She's fourteen for Christ's sake. Grown out of hide and seek!" Maureen shouted up the stairs.

"It's just a routine procedure Mrs. Webber. Is this her room, Mr

Webber?"

"You'll have to excuse the wife she's a bit..."

"I understand, sir. Did your daughter keep a diary?"

That night they slept as far as possible from each other in their not so large double bed. Breakfast television had a feature on the dangers of internet chat-rooms. The police officer had asked about that too. Roy took his wife up a cup of tea.

"Ever the peacemaker aren't you?" She reached out to hug her husband. "Where is she Roy? Do you think she's...?"

"Of course she isn't. Now get dressed you lazy cow and get my breakfast." He managed to get out of the bedroom before he started crying.

The first reporters had arrived at mid-morning. Soon the grass verges would become expanses of mud. Neighbours, whom Roy and Maureen had scarcely seen let alone knew, called to ask if there was anything they could do. The first bulletins had gone out on local radio already. At lunchtime the nation was informed by the first television reports. Journalists jostled at the school gates. It was amazing how many best friends Sally had. CCTV footage from nearby stations and the local shopping centre was busily scrutinised. A family liaison officer had been appointed and soon knew where the best biscuits were kept in the kitchen. A full description of Sally had been circulated. Maureen had deliberated over which photo to give to the police. The most recent one had been taken at her cousin's wedding a few months back. Somehow Sally looked too knowing, she thought it gave the wrong impression. Instead, she handed over the school one from last term. Both Maureen and Roy's bosses had said the right things when they had phoned that morning. The words of the sentences, 'If there's anything I can do' and 'I'm sure she's fine' had lost their meaning.

Roy's sister, Mary, arrived just after lunchtime. She assumed full control of the telephone and became official gatekeeper. All callers would now have to go through her. Roy had been hopeless at remembering what Sally had been wearing.

"He'd have trouble recalling what colour dress I got married in," Maureen said to Mary. The policewoman laughed as she dunked her third Hobnob. The television had been turned off by Mary. Roy pottered away in his greenhouse. *Best to keep myself busy,* he told himself as he watered his geranium cuttings.

Maureen found it strange that her sister-in-law was not giving her usual lecture on the dangers of cigarettes and the evils of passive smoking. It usually wound her up but now she would welcome that little bit of normality. Mary had even offered to go out and get some for her but Maureen had plenty left from the guy who sold them cheap down the club.

Sally had not been gone more than twenty-four hours. They hadn't argued, no change in behaviour recently. She knew most mums said it but her Sally was a good girl. If anything, Maureen had wished she had gone out more. She didn't have a steady boyfriend but you never told your parents everything, did you?

"Knew I should have bought her that mobile."

"Don't blame yourself Maureen," said her sister-in-law, who was coming towards her for a hug. "I'm sure there's a rational explanation for it all. We'll all be laughing about it this time next-"

"Well you go ahead and laugh your head off. It's not your daughter who's gone missing."

"I'm sorry I was only trying to help. If you don't want me here..."

"What's all this about?" Roy asked as he came back into the lounge. Maureen, Mary and the police officer all avoided Roy's eyes. Maureen went upstairs and slammed the bedroom door.

That afternoon a case conference was convened at the Webber's home. It was a grand title for going over the events of the last twenty-four hours and asking Sally's parents the same questions. The lead inspector suggested that a press conference would be standard practice.

"The drawback is that we then get all sorts of nutters and saddos phoning in with details of sightings and confessions. That's why we've held a few details back from the media."

Roy and Maureen nodded grimly. Maureen had never felt so passive in her life. Everything was happening to her and she had control over nothing. They were just waiting for what the police called a substantial lead. In a way the process seemed too familiar from television dramas and news broadcasts.

When the police had gone, Mary took control of the evening meal, inquiring of the permanent police presence whether she liked sprouts or not. Maureen and Roy took the opportunity to be alone together in their bedroom.

"You know you're the main suspect. They always think it's the father. That's what people are going to think. How are we going to...?"

Maureen didn't stop because of an interruption from her husband or a look of reproach. Instead he was looking at himself in the mirror. She reached out to hold his hand but he got up and went to the bathroom.

The press conference the next day had an unreal quality. They had decided that Roy would do the talking. Maureen sat by him. Tears were inevitable. As soon as she started, the flashes from the cameras went berserk. It's obviously what they expected from her. Over the next few days they were kept informed of possible leads and developments. Mary became the buffer between them and the rest of the world. Reporters were outdoing themselves to come up with a new angle. The headlines in the papers continued. Possible links with other disappearances kept circulations high. Maureen felt guilty for not losing her appetite. She had even managed to sleep. It did not stop her from looking dreadful though.

The call came after six days. Roy was accompanied to a nearby piece of wasteland about a mile and a half away. He identified Sally's clothing and then her body which had been shrouded within a hastily erected tent. Over the next forty-eight hours hundreds of police officers were called in from other forces to respond to the public pressure to find who had done this. Maureen would sit for hours in her daughter's bedroom. She wished she'd taken more photographs of her or recorded her voice. Mary assumed control of the funeral arrangements. She sat with her brother in the kitchen.

"You don't think she'd do anything stupid, do you? You've got plenty of sleeping pills and paracetemol in the bathroom."

Roy didn't answer.

Mary had given up asking about favourite hymns. She decided

herself. The Prime Minister had been questioned in the House about the return of the death penalty by their local MP. Several tabloids whipped up enthusiasm and the search was on for the monster who had done this. At a time when they most needed comfort Roy and Maureen were unable to help each other. They didn't argue. In fact they were more polite than usual. They were just cold. Mary had the mawkish collection of flowers on the grass verge redirected to old peoples' homes and hospitals.

"Somebody should get the benefit from them," she kept on saying. The burnt out tea-lights, hand-written poems and cuddly toys began to look pathetic in the drizzle.

On the afternoon before the funeral Roy was informed that the police had taken a local man into custody. It was to be kept away from the media while he was being interviewed but there was a DNA match. It took about an hour and a half for the news to be leaked. Mary had hoped that this would bring some sort of comfort to Roy and Maureen. Surely it was the not knowing why or who which had hurt the most; closure at last.

The dog-walker who had found the body had her fifteen minutes of fame. Speculation about motives and what had happened to Sally in the last hours and minutes of her life continued. The next few months were a blur for Maureen. On one level she coped. But it wasn't real. She was sleepwalking through her own life. It was like she was watching a film rather than being one of the central characters. She soon tired of the pity in the eyes of friends. She had been bombarded with advice: move, throw yourself into work, get therapy, take Prozac, succumb to religion.

None of these seemed to fit. She felt guilty that she had not used her personal nightmare to try and redeem something positive from the experience. She had been asked to appear on *Trisha* but she could not face it. Shouldn't she join or spearhead a government task force? Why didn't she set up a support group for families of murder victims or campaign for legal reform? It had all made no sense at all. No connection had been made between Sally and her killer. Danny Price had confessed in the light of what the police had called 'overwhelming evidence'.

The trial brought up the sense of loss and pointlessness which the funeral should have buried. God, she even thought in clichés now. She'd heard that many over the last few months. Although they put up a united front in the glare of flash photography as they entered and exited the court Roy and Maureen lived separate lives at home. They didn't even eat together. There had been no scenes or dramas; just a realisation that they no longer worked.

Maureen found herself staring at Mrs. Price in the courtroom. She seemed a pleasant enough woman. She had been called to the witness box. Yes, her Danny had always been a shy lad. Did his Gran's shopping. No, didn't have many friends. Liked to spend time on his own on the computer. Wasn't that common these days? The press would have loved the mothers to meet and even better still to have Maureen lay into her and then break down on the court steps. It never happened. Danny was sentenced and driven away to prison in the police van. Maureen had not recognised any of the people who swore at the blanketed figure. Roy held her hand. She didn't have the energy or cruelty to reject it, but it gave her no comfort. She just accepted it limply.

Danny did not take to prison life. He wet the bed the first night. By the second day he was sick of jokes about having the piss taken out of him, which the staff actively encouraged. Due to the high media profile of the murder he could not conceal the nature of his crime. The inquest into his death was carried out in a business like fashion. He had fallen and broken his neck. No witnesses. Nobody campaigned for greater prisoner safety. Mrs. Price and her mother were the only mourners at the funeral, which miraculously had been kept secret from the press. The service was conducted in a perfunctory manner. His mother and grandmother were still trying to make sense of the events of the last few months. Like Maureen and Roy they had stopped reading the papers or watching news or topical discussion programmes. They felt sufficient guilt without strangers pinning the blame on them too.

Maureen longed for the state of being 'united in grief' with Roy. But she waited in vain. Whatever they had together was gone. Time may be a healer, as she was frequently told by well-meaning but highly irritating people, but she did not have a couple of millennia to spare. He had returned to work. "Best to keep yourself busy," Mary would chime in regularly. Like she knew? Maureen gave up the pretence of returning to work and was prescribed a succession of tranquillisers by her GP. Not one of them managed to desensitise her enough. Sometimes a permanent vegetative state seemed an appealing option. To not feel. To not care. Therapists had dwelt on the last few days of Sally's life. They harked on about closure. One suggested a ritual where she could let go of the 'what ifs'. Candles would be lit, she would cut a cord which marked a perimeter around Sally's belongings. *What a load of bollocks!* she thought.

*****

Twenty odd years later, Maureen was living on the South Coast in a bungalow, which had had a seaview when it was built. They had moved after Roy's retirement. He'd joined the local bowls club and had promptly died of a heart attack four months to the day of him giving up work. Maureen felt entirely displaced now. She took up volunteering at a local charity shop on Monday and Friday mornings. She didn't have to worry about money as long as she was careful. Roy had provided well for her. One of the first things she had sold at the shop had been Roy's bowls whites.

"Almost new these," she'd said to the lucky shopper. "A real bargain."

It would have been quite out of character for Maureen to disclose how she had known. She had made a life's work out of avoiding sympathy and she was not about to start now. As she placed them in a supermarket carrier she chatted about the weather.

At home, which did not really feel like one, she did very little. She had a few nodding acquaintances. She did not keep in contact with any family members and friends had simply given up on her as she had never returned calls. It suited her this way. She read. She did not discriminate about books. Anything would do. The only reason she worked just two mornings at the charity shop was that these were unpopular shifts. Nobody wanted to volunteer for Monday morning as you had to deal with all the rubbish which had been dumped in the doorway over the weekend. It never bothered Maureen having to sift through all this. She knew now to wear rubber gloves for this task. Many of the old dears were pretty squeamish. She sometimes caught sight of herself in the mirror and hardly recognised what she saw. At fifty-seven she was by far the youngest volunteer. But she could pass for seventy. It's not as if she had given up on her appearance after becoming a widow. Her looks had been in long term decline ever since her daughter's death. The most dramatic change had been her colour hair as if the pillow-cases contained bleach. Her skin had forgotten how to stretch. When asked about her grandchildren she would abruptly change the subject.

One Friday morning she was working in the shop as usual. She liked to rearrange the blouses in alphabetical colour order. She enjoyed the fact that no-one else would know her rationale. She had a thing about wire hangers and went about exchanging them whenever she could. She was releasing a beige mac from one when she came in. Unmistakable. They had never met in the technical sense before, although Maureen had spent whole days concentrating on this woman's profile. Tracing the lines and bone structure, checking for similarities with her murdering son. Now here she was, looking at a set of pyrex bowls. Maureen knew her type; seeking out conversation even when unnecessary.

"How much are these love?" pretending that the price sticker was invisible. Maureen had not been recognised. Sure, time had passed but you wouldn't forget. Would you? Maureen avoided eye contact and remained monosyllabic. Mrs. Price wasn't really interested in the kitchenware, just lonely. One was the mother of a monster, one was the mother of an angel. One was to blame and one was to be pitied. Outsiders could easily sit in judgment. Grief had transformed their appearances more than time. This meeting could have triggered a tabloid bidding frenzy. Maureen could have chosen to say something. But she didn't.

A few moments later, alone in the shop, Maureen is on her hands and knees. She is sweeping up the shards of glass and pieces of pyrex with a dustpan and brush. It's funny, she's usually so careful with things.

Miniature Catflap

It made such a lot of dust. Protective sheets would have been a good idea. I had the bit well and truly between my teeth, or more accurately, in my drill.

I have chosen my time well. I certainly know their routines. Their comings and goings are recorded in my notebook. I have developed a rudimentary code, never using their names, just in case it is discovered. The younger child is at a state run nursery. The teenager attends a secondary school, whose hours were somewhat relaxed. Their mother is on some sort of course, the purpose of which is to make her more attractive to potential employers. Quite frankly, a bath once in a while might do the trick more effectively. I have feigned interest at times in their tawdry lives, whenever she has struck up a pavement conversation. No wonder my pension is so meagre. I seem to be single-handedly paying for their education and her benefits. The boyfriend is another class act. He is wastrel personified. He drifts in and out of her life.

Last night they had a blazing row. It began at 7:14 and he stormed out at 8:47. This ensures that he will be away for some days; thirteen is the current record. He is not the type to turn up on her doorstep with a bunch of red roses, even if his dole cheque stretched that far.

So, this morning I am safe to carry out my project. I had done some research. The lady at the library had not been terribly helpful. I am sure that whatever qualifications she amassed were not NVQs or degrees in charm. I discovered a manual on masonry drilling so was aware of the possible pitfalls. My visit to the hardware shop was illuminating. I think that I presented myself as being a knowledgeable DIY fanatic as I read out my requirements: an electric drill with an extensive range of accessories. I think that I impressed the owner. One of my greatest fears was about hitting a pipe or cable, so I forked out a substantial amount on an electronic detector. It may come in handy again in the future.

I practised with my drill on a variety of materials. It went through a brick remarkably quickly. The handle felt reassuringly solid. It was my first experience of power tools. Why had I left it so late in life? This must be what it feels like to hold a revolver.

I had already calculated the optimal place to begin my task. I sit myself down on the staircase leading to the first floor and turn on the drill. If the dividing wall is greater than fourteen and a half inches then my drilling would be in vain.

I have the nozzle attachment of the vacuum cleaner close to me and suck up the brick dust every couple of inches. It would be so much easier to have another person to assist. But who could I trust? It takes less time than I imagined. My mug of tea is still too hot for me to drink.

I am nothing if I am not methodical. I rewind the flex of the drill and replace all the attachments. They fit neatly into their own compartments. I return the extension cable into its usual coiled snake formation and then put the hoover away in the cupboard under the stairs. I then reach for the keys. My neighbour has been a little too trusting; I hold her spare set in case of emergencies. I have had to come to the rescue in the past when her slack jawed son came home early from school with a highly suspicious migraine, having mislaid his keys. Quite why he thought that listening to ridiculous, thumping, tuneless music at deafening levels would prove beneficial is beyond me.

I let myself into her home after a last minute cursory check. Her car is not outside. I know that she is attending an all day course, both children are at school and the boyfriend is temporarily off the scene. The smell is rather overpowering. She may be on a modest income, yet surely supermarket brand cleaning products and air fresheners are within her budget. The house is a mirror image of my own in lay out and dimensions. Otherwise, there is no comparison. I do not class myself as obsessively house proud but the state of this home would certainly prompt the slackest of social workers to consider taking both offspring into care. The carpet is of an indeterminate colour. I am unable to work out whether it is patterned or severely stained. I arrive well-prepared. I have a small satchel with me, containing necessary items. I have thought this through thoroughly. Fail to plan, plan to fail is my maxim. I avoid entering the kitchen. Who knows what horrors lurk there. It is not difficult to locate the small patch of brick dust which I caused at the top of the staircase. I pull out my dustpan and brush. The hole itself is only a quarter of an inch in diameter and could possibly avoid detection, considering all the scuffs, dents and gashes that already feature on every wall. She must host regular kick boxing competitions for the house to have sustained so much damage. Nevertheless, I cut out a small square of wallpaper from behind a mirror with my Stanley knife. I then glue the top part so that it covers the newly-created aperture. I am impressed with my handiwork. It acts as a miniature catflap.

At the bottom of the stairs, I look back to check and am pleased to see that there is no trace of my visit. If I am spotted or even challenged as I lock the door I will simply claim that I heard a strange noise and that I was investigating; what a model neighbour I would appear to be.

This afternoon I shall peruse a fascinating book I have just bought. It's all about poisonous gases.

Imagined Tenderness

At least he had the good grace to seem a little embarrassed. He was out of his depth. He knew that platitudes were redundant. I steered him through the short meeting. We stuck to safe topics. Wasn't it shocking how short the Great British public's memory was? Booting out our national Saviour like that! Churchill had won the war for us, what price gratitude now? That sort of thing. I suppose I should have cared about the perilous course our country was taking. He was probably new in the job. Well, he'd better toughen up. There's plenty worse than me. I wonder how the white collar fastens at the back of his neck? He said he'd pray for me. I pretended that would be a comfort and let him go.

The quiet returned to my room. I don't think I was feeling sorry for myself. Self-pity is so terribly unattractive in a person. Possibly inspired by this uncalled for Christian intervention I began to count my blessings. Hadn't we been urged to do this at Sunday School? The list was not overly long. At least my parents had not lived to see me like this. Spanish Influenza had carried them off at the end of 'the war to end all wars'. I suppose in time we would learn to call it the First World War. My cousins, who were poor excuses for siblings, were sorry for me but could do nothing for me. Their visits had evaporated. Also I hadn't lost my mind. I resisted the logic that if I had then how would I know I had. Therein lies madness, literally. The view from my room was tolerable. I'd never been much of a nature lover. I was very much of the opinion that once you'd seen one tree you'd seen them all. But at least it gave my dwindling trickle of visitors something to talk about.

One of the doctors had the burning conviction that if I regularly attended rehabilitation sessions then there was a chance I would regain sensation in my legs, perhaps even walk again. I went along with him out of plain good manners, rather than faith in the medical profession. When I could bear to look at them, which was not often, my lifeless legs seemed like sticks. They didn't feel like part of me. That's a ridiculous thing to say. They didn't feel anything; that was the trouble. I'd long tired of my party trick of pricking them with a needle or pin. Sometimes I had not known when to stop and matron had sternly reminded me of the persistent nature of blood stains. That was me told!

I'd become an absolute genius on the subject of sport. Anyone who had known me previously, would have thought that the blast had done something to my brain after all. As an adolescent, I had shown neither the slightest inclination nor proficiency in anything approaching the physical. The only exercise my body had enjoyed in adulthood was the daily battle against the devious minds who set the crosswords in the higher brow daily newspapers. The delicious irony had not escaped me that now my body was good for nothing, my mind was crammed full of facts about all aspects of sport. I had a constant craving for more. As I had no personal preference I could not be selective. I cast my net wide in the collection of information about human achievement. My doctor saw in my obsession a signal that I was showing a keen interest in the world outside my hospital room. Poppycock! Let him think that if he chooses. I had, what some would think as, far baser motives. I was intent on setting a sprat to catch a mackerel. His name was Harry.

Every morning, Harry popped into my room to exchange pleasantries. After a few weeks we had exhausted the topic of weather, and current affairs were of little interest to either of us. He seemed a man of few words but when I asked to borrow his paper I was dismayed to discover it was a newspaper devoted utterly to horse racing. I did not know that newspapers like this existed. He came back later that morning to collect it. I feigned interest. He mistook my gratitude for a genuine love of sport. I wasn't quite sure what Harry did exactly in the hospital and after our daily chats became a regular fixture of my day, it would have been rude to ask. Before the war he was not the kind of person I would have generally spoken to, unless it was to issue orders. I surreptitiously began to subscribe to a range of sporting journals and avidly read the back pages of papers until I could confidently engage in sporting banter. It helped to make sense of pre-war conversations in my local barbershop, which along with the scissors, had gone over my head. It amused me to ask "Who do you fancy for the Cup?" and actually have an opinion.

As the weather improved, it was thought to be beneficial to my recovery if I spent time in the hospital gardens. Due to a dearth of able-bodied men, Harry seemed glad enough to assist in lifting me out of bed and into my wheel chair. The first few times, he treated me rather roughly and I felt like a sack of potatoes. I tried to disguise my discomfort and hoped that he did not catch me wincing. Rather like the senses of a blind person overcompensate in other areas, so my upper body felt every bump on the short journey in my new means of transport. I learned to ask Harry open-ended questions and nodded sagely as he proffered his opinions. This meant more time together. I don't think many people had listened to him so intently. I felt it was a fair transaction. He obviously benefited from having such an appreciative audience. I had stopped pretending to myself that all I got out of the experience was the altruistic feeling of boosting his feeling of self-worth.

I think what surprised me most was my lack of guilt. I loved the smell of him. It was a heady mixture of Woodbines and grease. I was always a little disappointed whenever he had washed his hands before he came to visit. I was aware that it was not a meeting of minds. It was a purely physical attraction. I liked the way he moved. It sounds pathetic but I would often ask him to fetch things from the other side of the room just so I could watch him. He was not particularly graceful. If he had been, that may have detracted from his appeal. The most precious memory of Harry is when he peeled an orange for me. A simple thing, but the combination of his large hands unused to handling this rare fruit, appealed to me. I had no worries about my excitement revealing my true motives for wanting to spend so much time with him. I had no sensation below the pyjama waist band. It was erotic in an academic way. If I could have done something about it, then I think I would have lost interest. It was the hopelessness of the situation which provided the thrill.

After an absence of a few days I plucked up the courage to ask matron where Harry was. Apparently he had moved with his wife and his young family over a hundred miles away. There was no note. No explanation. Nothing like that. After all we were men. All that remained was a lingering regret.

Reading is Bad for Your Health

I can hear snatches of conversations – "I don't know what made him do it" and "Quite out of character." I'll let them think I'm still asleep. I'll keep my eyes closed. They're bound to go away soon and give me some peace. But they stay put as if they've taken root. I suppose I should be grateful that my sisters have come to my hospital bedside. There are precious few other people queuing up at this time to offer support. But there's a price I'm going to have to pay for their family loyalty. I shall never hear the end of it. I wish the sedatives they've given me would kick in.

*****

The Mickey Finns must have done the trick. I open my eyes. It's dark I've got no idea of the time but at least the *Sisters of No Mercy* have left. I'll have to face them later but at least I have a respite, however brief. I start to piece together the events of the past few days. I remember something about a book. Was I buying one? There's somebody outside my room. I close my eyes as they enter. She's wearing a uniform, but it's not a doctor or nurse. It's a policewoman. I think for a minute that there's some sort of fancy dress party going on. Perhaps the Village People will appear. I don't think I'm as lucid as I thought.

She sits next to me and leans over. "I've come to ask you a few questions. Is it OK if I call you by your first name?"

I nod and she continues. "Well, Roger, I'd like to find out from you about the incident in the high street yesterday afternoon."

There is a pause. I think she is worried that I've fallen asleep. "If you can tell me in your own words what happened...?"

"It's all rather hazy. There's something about a book that seems important but I can't for the life of me think why it's so significant."

Another person comes into my room. This one is wearing a white coat. She's looking furiously at the policewoman. "What on Earth are you doing here? You've no right to be in this room. My patient has suffered a great trauma to his head and needs rest. He's in no fit state to answer any questions."

"But I'm following up on our enquiries about the alleged crime committed yesterday afternoon and I need to ask–"

"Your questions can wait until my patient has recovered. His injuries are potentially serious."

There is a short stand-off and I'm unsure who will metaphorically blink first. Finally, the policewoman stands up and leaves the room. There are no more words spoken until she has closed the door behind her. The doctor apologises for the interruption and assures me that hospital security will ensure that I shan't be interviewed by the police until she gives permission. "You need rest and plenty of it. The police can wait. You're not going anywhere soon. I'll ask a nurse to give you something to help you sleep."

I thank her and try to scratch my head. I've got an itch and I am desperate to relieve it. It takes a considerable amount of effort to raise my arm but I eventually manage. I get a shock when my fingers don't come into contact with my forehead. Instead they are touching material I trace it around my scalp and discover that my entire head is bandaged.

She stands over me and explains. "You had a nasty bump when you head hit the pavement. If you ask me, I think the police were rathe heavy handed. We've given you a head scan and the signs are encouraging but we intend to monitor you closely. There is always the possibility of a clot caused by the impact with the paving stones tha don't always show up on the MRI."

I want to ask her for details but she's gone. It's strange really that want to find out from her what happened to me yesterday. After all, was the one who was there and she wasn't. Or was she? Could there b some massive coincidence in the fact that she was there and is a ke witness? My headache is excruciating. It's as if the actual effort dredging up details from my foggy memory is causing it. I fumble f some sort of bell or alarm to request a painkiller when a member staff enters with a small plastic medicine cup. He hands them to me an gestures towards a beaker of water that is on my table. I try to pick it but my hand seems to go through it. My coordination is shot to bi After several failed attempts by me, he picks it up for me and places to my lips. The pills are difficult to swallow. He helps me to sit up bed and after a supreme effort on my part, they go down. It doesn't ta long for them to take effect. I feel woozy and the room really does seem to spin around. Maybe this is what LSD is like. I'm not worried. It's quite a pleasant sensation and at least the headache's going.

*****

When I wake up, it's daylight outside. Already I'm unsure which day of the week it is. I hope they don't send a doctor in to do some sort of mental assessment on me as I'd be totally incapable of answering the simplest of questions. They'd ship me off to some sort of psychiatric wing where my jacket would be done up from behind.

The same doctor appears and asks how I'm feeling.

"Still a bit groggy but the headache's not so bad. Trying to make sense of everything that's happened."

"Don't worry. Everything will eventually slot into place. The human body is remarkably resilient and the brain is no exception. You just need time to heal. You've become quite a celebrity."

She's left the room before I'm able ask what she meant by that comment. God, I didn't kill somebody, did I? I would be a flaky suspect in court. I would answer 'I can't remember' to any questions the prosecution team put to me. I'd probably get my name wrong.

I've been left alone for the morning. I drift in and out of sleep. I've endured the indignity of using a bedpan already and am fighting the need for it again. I'm hoping I'll have the strength to hobble to the lavatory when the need arises. A tray of lunch is brought in to me. I pick at a few things but the action of picking things up with my fork is literally hit and miss. I use my fingers. I am munching my way through a roast potato when the doctor reappears.

"Good to see your appetite has returned. That's always a good sign. Visiting times are pretty relaxed here. One of your sisters would like to come and see you. I wanted to check with you if that's alright?"

"Which one is it?"

From the doctor's description I figure I will be safe. It's the younger of the two. I can just about cope with her. I then rather imperiously say to the doctor, "Send her in." Fortunately she has a sense of humour and salutes and asks whether I have any other orders for her before she goes.

Jenny comes into my room, heavily laden with gifts. She sits next to me. There is a slight peck on my cheek. We don't go in for big public displays of affection in our family. I can see that she's trying to hold back the tears.

"I bet you all thought I was a goner."

"Don't joke about it Roger. You almost scared us to death." She then pauses with embarrassment when she realises the inappropriate turn of phrase she's used.

Jenny busies herself with looking for a vase for the lilies she's brought for me.

"Aren't they for dead people?"

Again, she turns red and asks if she should dispose of them. I tell her I'm only kidding but nevertheless it is a rather strange choice of flower.

"I've brought you some magazines for when you're feeling better and up to reading. The doctor told me that you wouldn't be up to that quite yet. She was telling me about the muscles in your eyes needing to heal and that you may not be able to see properly for a few more days."

That explains my constant dizziness and the impression that I'm looking through a kaleidoscope at times. "Well I'm glad *you're* being told something. What else did she have to say for herself? All she told me was that I've become quite a celebrity. Whatever's that supposed to mean?"

"Surely you remember what happened?"

I think it might be churlish to point out that I wouldn't be asking her for information if I have perfect recall of events. When she realises that I'm not joking and that I do not know what happened, she clears her throat and I can tell I'm in for a long story.

"Well it started with Mr Cleminson."

"What's my neighbour got to do with it?"

"He's just had a hip operation and you promised to take his library book back for him. He was getting all worked up about getting a fine."

"I knew it had something to do with a book."

Jenny gives me one of her teachery looks that makes it clear that further interruptions will not be tolerated. She takes a deep breath and continues. "You drove to the library and popped in to return the book. And when you came back to your car there was a traffic warden writing you out a ticket. You then went on to reason with him that you had only been inside the library for five minutes. This had no effect on the traffic warden. You then went for a subtler approach by appealing to the warden's better nature. You carefully explained that you were doing a favour for a sick neighbour. The warden said that it was out of his hands, parking on double yellow lines was illegal and that since he had begun to write the penalty ticket he had to continue. It could have been at this point that you called him a Nazi. This wasn't a good call as the warden was Jewish."

I'm aware that I'm blushing and want her to stop. But I want to learn how I managed to end up in this hospital bed. So I bite my tongue and let her continue. It's like hearing about a stranger.

"Then after he threatened to call the police, you accused him of bullying and questioned whether we lived in a free society. You'd drawn quite a crowd by this stage. It was unclear what he said that made you grab him around the neck. A passing police officer instructed you to remove your hands from his throat. You refused and unfortunately the local force was using tasers as part of crime prevention pilot scheme. You were temporarily stunned and fell and hit your head."

"How on Earth do you know all this, Jenny? Please don't tell me that my own sister was there and didn't do anything to help."

"You've gone viral."

She pulls out her smartphone and shows me a YouTube clip. It's titled *Fifty year old man loses it with traffic warden.*

"You've clocked up over two million hits already. A passer-by recorded it. Listen to this. The sound quality's not that great."

Unfortunately I can make out most of my lunatic rants about police states and mindless bureaucracy. I must have been really losing the plot to claim that I was being persecuted for being a Good Samaritan. When the doctor comes back I'll ask her if it's possible to die of shame.

Narcissine Attraction

"You simply must meet Lionel. You'll love him. He used to be 'T[
Nose' for Givenchy. That's before he launched his own fragrance
course."

I racked my not inconsiderable brain. I was trying to figure out ho[
Lionel's olfactory prowess could endear him to me. Friends can [
quite strange. I smiled.

"I can't wait." I hoped I sounded convincing.

Then my hostess was off, working the room and I was left by t[
fireplace. I knew nobody except Daphne and even she was just [
gossiping acquaintance I'd known through the tennis club. That's fro[
the days when I could handle a racquet. I was formidable on the court
those days. Nowadays, bowls is more my style. That's when I can [
bothered to get out of bed.

Daphne's clock marched to a different beat to that of the Greenwi[
Meridian. I could have sworn it said ten past eight half an hour ago. Y[
somehow the minute hand has only struggled around to the four. I w[
calculating how much longer I need to endure this dullness when[
young man approached. He had the smile of a simpleton.

"Hello Uncle Gerry. I expect you don't remember me." He put out [
right hand towards me in an extremely forthright fashion.

"Dear boy, it's super to see you again." I couldn't for the life of me think who he was. Fortunately he put me out of my misery. Apparently I was his godfather. There have been so many godchildren over the years that all the christenings blur into one. I was the obvious choice for many of my friends. No children of my own and although not in the *Times Rich List*, I was comfortable. I'm sure that some of my friends expected me to croak anytime soon and leave my fortune to their pride and joy. I intended to disappoint.

"You certainly have a tight grip young man."

"I've just completed my officer's training. Sorry if I hurt you."

"Good grief man. I may look fragile but I can withstand a handshake. What on earth is a young man like you doing here with all of us old crocks?"

I scanned the room to check on my initial recollection. I was correct. The average age must be about sixty-five.

"Well, Daphne is my fiancée's aunt. To be honest, it's a flying visit as we are having supper with friends later and I was meant to meeting Vanessa here. She's running late. It was probably her hair. She always wants to be just so."

"Congratulations on the engagement. It only seems like yesterday when–"

Luckily I was spared dredging up the memory of one of his childhood misdemeanours. To be brutally frank I wasn't certain I could even recall any. Vanessa chose that exact moment to arrive.

She gave her fiancé a fulsome kiss that in my day would have been reserved for when they were alone. "So sorry I was late, Seb. I just couldn't decide what to wear and the phone just wouldn't stop ringing and I daren't put it on silent in case you were trying to contact me."

Ah, Sebastian. I was grateful she'd name-checked him. I had distant memories of him as a baby in a ridiculous baptismal gown and an appalling string of middle names, so as not to offend either side of the family. Then she turned towards me and the smile possessed the strength of heavy duty floodlights.

"I'm glad you haven't been all alone. Do introduce me to your friend."

He did as he was told and she lied exquisitely.

"So you're Uncle Gerry. I've heard so much about you."

This can't possibly have been true. I featured so scarcely in the lives of any of my godchildren. I had made the forgetting of birthdays an art form. But I joined in the charade.

"Congratulations to you both. When I'd heard that somebody had agreed to make an honest man of young Sebastian I was intrigued to meet her. And now I see this vision of pulchritude before me. I can't believe his good fortune. He must have done something exceedingly good in a previous life. Have you set a date yet?"

Vanessa despatched Sebastian in search of drinks for all of us and then went into the minutest of detail about her oncoming nuptial arrangements. This type of talk normally can be relied upon to bore me to tears, but for some strange reason I felt drawn to her descriptions of bridesmaids' dresses and table decorations. She was charm personified. I was enchanted. She suggested to Sebastian that he should circulate as she was wanting to monopolise me 'since it wasn't every day one met such a fascinating man'. I customarily do not fall for such naked flattery. But on this occasion I was under her spell. She was so easy to be with. I encouraged her to talk. I considered the prospect of her departure for a late supper with profound sadness. Oh dear. I hope I wasn't becoming one of those pathetic elderly people who develop inappropriate crushes on people a mere fraction of their own age.

"But Gerry, I've done all the talking. Tell me a little of yourself. Apart for providing a sterling role model for Sebastian throughout his formative years, what do you do with your time?"

When I'm asked this question I invariably lie. I usually say that I paint or write poetry. I talk up the small amount of charity work that I've done in the past. It puts people off the scent. But for some reason I felt compelled to be utterly truthful to Vanessa.

"I've rather wasted my life. I've no children and never stuck at a career long enough to succeed. I've been cursed with enough money to not have to do anything. I've rather allowed myself to fritter away my time. I regret that I haven't left my mark."

Tears had formed in my eyes. Vanessa didn't respond with embarrassment or rapidly change the subject. After a suitable pause she took my hand and simply smiled at me. I took a deep breath and determined to change the subject.

"Enough of all this maudlin stuff. Tell me more about you."

She went on to recount her childhood and that her family called her the foundling as she was so much taller than her younger siblings and resembled neither her father nor mother. School in her words had been 'such fun'. She hadn't minded about boarding. I wish I could have bottled her enthusiasm for life. I asked about their honeymoon. Apparently Sebastian was entitled to some form of extended leave and they planned to tour the world. Some sort of ticket that meant as long as they kept travelling eastwards they were alright. When I showed my anxiety about the lack of plans for accommodation, she took my hand again. "You're so sweet. You mustn't worry. We'll be fine. Besides I'll have my personal soldier boy with me."

Again, she laughed as she spoke. I found the sound entrancing. Sebastian chose that moment to come up to us.

"I'm sorry Uncle, but I'm going to have to whisk Vanessa off for supper. We're going to be late as it is."

Vanessa pulled a face of great displeasure as if being parted from me was a torment. It was kind of her.

"Just stop calling me Uncle, will you? I'm old enough to be Methuseleh's brother but I don't want to be reminded of the fact by a whippersnapper like you."

"OK...Gerry. That's going to be tricky for me."

Vanessa hugged me goodbye and said, "Well Gerry, I'm delighted that we met. I know it sounds daft but I feel as if I've known you for years. I will accept no excuses...you are coming to our wedding and that's final. And if you ask nicely I shall place you next to all the eligible single women."

And then she was gone. The glare of her bright smile was left. I must have been standing watching the door where she'd left when Daphne approached.

"Lovely girl, isn't she? I've watched her grow up and turn into quite a lady. Sebastian'll have his hands full. But of course, you're his godfather. So you'll all be kind of related. Funny that, because Vanessa's my niece. You remember my little brat of a sister, surely? She was rather fond of you, if I recall. I think she had crazy notions of getting hitched to you. You spent a great deal of time together. But I managed to talk her out of it that summer. I told her you were far too old for her. Age gap marriages seldom work. I was her big sister and could always boss her about. Then she had one of those whirlwind romances and was married within the month. Three children within five years. Touch and go whether it was the full nine months from the wedding day. I just remember Papa being happy she had a ring on her finger. What's wrong with you, you've gone dreadfully pale?'

I feigned a sudden headache and said I was prone to them recently.

"That's such a shame. I was hoping to introduce you to Lionel. He's such a card. But you really don't look that good. Can I call a doctor or something? At least have a little sit down. I don't like the idea of you going home alone."

"I'll be fine, Daphne. I just need some fresh air. It's been a lovely evening, I wouldn't have missed it for the world."

Daphne rushed off to track down my coat, scarf and hat. Mercifully she did that quickly. I pecked her on the cheek, promising to call her as soon as I arrived home.

"I certainly don't want to imagine you being found unconscious in the gutter. I'm rather cross with Vanessa monopolising you this evening. I shall call her tomorrow and tear her off a strip. She's worn you out. We're not getting any younger, are we?"

I put on my outdoor clothing and went out into the cold. I wondered what type of wedding present I should buy. They would think it rather odd if I was overly generous.

It will be strange to see another man walk my daughter down the aisle.

Competitive Diagnosis

I wanted to prove myself. The interview, CV and qualifications ticked the medical boxes. I wanted my peers to know I was quick-witted and possessed a zany sense of humour. I'd recently taken up my post as a junior doctor at the local hospital when I spotted the poster in the staff canteen. I signed up on the spot. This was a month ago.

I spent some time in my cubbyhole of a room, when on-call, practising my off the cuff remarks and one-liners. It was quite an irritation when I was called upon to treat patients. I checked my deadpan facial expressions in the gents' lavatory mirror. I didn't want people to get the wrong idea about me, so I rationed my visits there.

The big day arrived and I helped set up the chairs in the small gym building used by the rehabilitation team. The local news team promised to call by as they liked the idea of medical staff participating in *Red Nose Day*. Charity and medicine went well together.

I was one of the doctors involved in a type of *What's My Line?* The medical twist meant that the pretend patients would describe their symptoms and we would have to diagnose their conditions using the least number of questions. If we asked more than ten questions the master of ceremonies had a huge custard pie destined to wipe the smile off our faces. I was determined to avoid this humiliation at all costs. I was here to impress.

I'd brushed up on my anatomical knowledge. Luckily I'd kept all my text books from my training days. They brought back the nights of black coffee fuelled cramming. There wasn't a bone on the human skeleton that I couldn't name. I always kept abreast of developments in my field as well as having a keen interest in scientific breakthroughs and new drug therapies.

Our names had been picked out of a hat to decide the running order. At that time, I didn't know whether I'd been cursed or blessed to be first in the running order. The senior registrar was running the show. She explained the rules to the audience. She encouraged the two hundred strong crowd to support all the contestants. I was introduced. She smiled briefly at me. She'd clearly forgotten the unfortunate incident when I'd made a joke about her totally unpronounceable name. I was a new member of staff, so it was hardly surprising that my entrance didn't receive a huge amount of applause. I was sure that the audience would warm up as the evening progressed.

I was asked to sit in the doctor's chair behind a desk that had been brought into the hall for the sake of authenticity. The first patient was introduced. It was one of the hospital porters. I'd already had several run-ins with him, citing my superiority when he had failed to carry out simple tasks I'd requested. Don't these people know how precious a doctor's time is? The crazy thing was that I'd ended up with a verbal warning on my record to avoid an undesirable disciplinary hearing so early in my career. His CBE and thirty year service award obviously intimidated the management. By the huge grin on his face I could see that he clearly didn't bear a grudge. After all, this was all in aid of charity. The registrar waited for the cheers to subside before she showed him to his seat opposite me, so that we were in profile to the audience.

The temporary stage lights were rather strong but I could pick out a few familiar faces in the front row. There was the extremely effeminate male nurse I'd joked with on my first day. He wasn't smiling the day we met so I asked him if it was his time of the month. Some people can be so touchy. He was sitting next to the most attractive nurse at the hospital. I'd asked her out a couple of times but I must have chosen the wrong nights as she was always busy. A woman from the cafeteria glared at me from the second row. I'd noticed she'd had a cold sore as she served my macaroni cheese. I'd only suggested she made an appointment at the sexually-transmitted disease clinic. She'd taken offence. Some people just don't have a sense of humour.

The porter sat and I was able to ask my first question. I'd read a backlog of issues of *The Lancet* and felt up to date with medical developments.

I enquired about his health and asked how I could help. I used my most solicitous voice. His reply caused a ripple of laughter.

"Baby, it's cold outside."

I was surprised at his informality when speaking to a doctor. But I let it slip. We're constantly being told to break down the *them and us* barriers. Even so, I didn't study for all those years to be spoken to like that. I went on to ask about his symptoms.

"I've got chills. They're multiplying."

I had to wait for the laughter to die down for him to be able to give me more information about his condition so that I could determine what the problem was.

"I'm all shook up."

I nodded sagely which seemed to provoke even more laughter. The registrar had to intervene. The poor woman was evidently suffering from allergies as her eyes were streaming at this point. It wasn't even hayfever season yet. I asked him to elaborate.

"I just don't know what to do with myself."

I asked if he had any chest pains and he enigmatically replied, "My heart will go on."

I asked whether he had a temperature.

"It's not unusual."

This wasn't a terribly helpful reply but it made the audience scream with laughter.

I decided to change tack. I asked him about his sleeping patterns. I couldn't quite catch his response as by this stage the audience were really entering into the spirit of the whole thing. There was so much noise that I could only make out something about having 'tears on his pillow'.

This made me consider a rare syndrome involving inflammation of the lacrimal glands. I would have pursued this further under normal circumstances but the registrar pointed out that I had a minute remaining. I would have had plenty more time if the audience had not been so rowdy.

I thought I'd be a little bit edgy and ask about his bowel movements and his regularity. I hoped this would wipe the impertinent smirk off his face. His response caused me to lose precious seconds as by this stage the audience was totally engaged and was roaring its approval. He'd only said 'Like a bat out of hell'. This seemed like a total non-sequitur.

The registrar announced that my time was up and I was given a final opportunity to diagnose my patient. There was an instant hush and I was only aware of my fast beating heart. My professional credibility was on the line. I felt I was nowhere near and I thought it better to explain that I needed more time to make an incorrect assertion. The porter was asked to reveal the nature of his medical complaint. He left a dramatic pause and then explained that his particular condition was that he was restricted solely speaking in song titles or lyrics. There was massive applause from the hall and delight when the custard pie was squashed into my face. But a rule's a rule and I took my just desserts. There were blinding flashes from mobiles and cameras as people queued to get a good shot of me with a shaving foamed face. I didn't know how popular I was. I must have made more of an impact than I'd thought in the workplace. I was congratulated on being such a good sport and for entering into the spirit of the event.

I didn't stay for the rest of the show. Strangers slapped me on the back as if I were some sort of folk hero. I went straight to my laptop and began to search for the name of this otherwise unheard of syndrome. I was astounded to discover no mention of it.

*****

It's now two o'clock in the morning. I've decided I'm going to apply for a research grant. If I'm lucky, this new syndrome might be named after me. Strange that I'd never heard of its symptoms before. I knew that tonight would be a success. I'll probably become more popular than ever.

Lightning Source UK Ltd.
Milton Keynes UK
UKOW04f1139040214

225839UK00002B/315/P

9 781906 657154